CRISIS
of
FAITH

CARRIE WATTS

hope*books
hopebooks.com
Because the world needs your hope-filled
words now more than ever.

"*Crisis of Faith* is a beautiful and honest picture that demonstrates the depth of suffering and the power of healing, both spiritually and emotionally. Young women who are acquainted with grief can find faith and hope for their own life through this story."

- Stephanie Wielgosz,
MA, LPC, BC-TMH

"Carrie Watts' *Crisis of Faith* is a poignant tale which focuses on delicate issues in a direct and loving manner. Watts is a formidable witness for our Lord and Savior, Jesus Christ, while weaving a fast-paced story which reveals spiritual truths and addresses earthly betrayals. You'll feel like you are a new Christian again as you consume Watts' words. A book to share."

- Konnie Risinger
BS K - 8th grade,
Masters in gifted education,
National Board Certified

"Carrie Watts' *Crisis of Faith* powerfully depicts the raw beauty of a fulfilled Kingdom-driven and Spirit-filled purpose. Through her masterful emphasis on the strength of prayer, the purity of good works overflowing from one's faith, and the reminder that like-minded friends produce good fruit, young women will find comfort, hope, and strength in the truth of Watts' words. A truly enchanting story that glorifies Christ!"

- Ansley Claire Strong
Founder of Tuesday Mornings Ministries
& a 2024 MS Christian Living Leader of the Future

TABLE OF CONTENTS

PROLOGUE

"Therefore I tell you, whatever you ask in prayer, believe that you have received it, and it will be yours." Mark 11:24

Dezzie stuffed her notebook in her backpack. "Faith, the phones aren't ringing, and I have so much to do before dinner. I'm going to sneak out a little early."

"What? You're leaving me here all alone?" I whined.

"Well, it is May 1st. Somebody has a birthday today," she said, winking and shooting me with her finger drawn like the rhinestone cowgirl. "The reservation is for six o'clock sharp."

"It's just us, right?" I looked her in the eye, begging her, "No surprises, Dezzie Diamond."

She smiled and pointed at me, saying, "Don't be late, Faith Joule."

Just as I placed the headset on, the phone rang.

"This is Faith at the Bright Light Safe House crisis hotline. How can I help you?"

Dezzie has been my friend since childhood. Our names reflect our aspirations. Faith embodies a belief in someone greater than ourselves, while desire signifies a heartfelt longing. Like many children, we had a faith that we were protected and a desire to help others who were not. At twelve years old, we made a vow, dedicating our lives as the neighborhood guardian angels. Now, at twenty-two, we have focused our efforts on aiding young girls who are fleeing from harm's grasp.

Yet, despite our lofty aspirations, we're still students – graduate students. Dezzie is pursuing law while I'm nearing the completion of my studies in child psychology. Fueled by a shared vision to provide a sanctuary for vulnerable young girls in need of a refuge, the Bright Light Safe House is our first stride towards making a local impact. Together, we sharpen one another's resolve like iron against iron.

CHAPTER 1

HOPE'S BRAVE ESCAPE

Hammers tapped and drills buzzed. Uninterrupted by the sound of progress in the distance, my fingers tapped the keys on my notebook computer. "May we rise above the noise to hear the voice that calls for help," I typed. Staring at the four walls in the tiny staff lounge at the Bright Light Safe House, I sat at a small round café table flanked by a refrigerator and a microwave, editing my latest addition to my master's thesis, titled "Heal Early: Don't Let Childhood Trauma Steal Another Minute of Your Life." I looked up at the ceiling and moved my neck side to side with outstretched arms in surrender, stretching and praying for the children who were in our care and for the ones who would seek shelter with us in the future. "Dear Jesus, my heart aches for the children who have been abused. Help me to help the young women who have lost their childlike faith so that they can heal and trust you."

Before I could utter "Amen," like a shot in the dark, I heard the freezer produce a tray of ice that fell like boulders into the empty bucket below. Startled, my body jumped when, simultaneously, a booming fist pounding, much louder, echoed through the back door.

Then I heard a voice. "Please open up!"

I sprinted to the back. Our security guard, who happens to be my brother Oliver, arrived with Gabby, the guard dog.

"Stand back, Faith," Oliver demanded as he opened the door. A young teen girl with a black baseball cap quickly forced herself inside and put her back against the wall. Her neck and head were as flat against it as if she was trying to become the wall itself.

"I need to hide. Please help me," she desperately begged us.

"Follow me," I urgently grabbed her hand as I led her straight to the admission counselor's office. "You'll be safe here. My name is Faith. I'll stay here with you."

She crawled behind the desk and crouched down. She grabbed her knees, pulled them in close to her chest, and tucked her head as if hoping to vanish from sight.

I felt stupid asking since it was obvious, but I asked anyway, as it would be the next question on a crisis call, "Are you running from danger?"

"Yes, I'm scared. He'll find me. He's close."

"How close is he?" I asked.

"He's one block away, down the street at the Quick Mart."

I quickly dialed 911 to request backup, my voice steady but urgent, "This is Faith Joule with the Bright Light Safe House. We have a victim here in the building who is in immediate danger. Her abuser is possibly following her and is nearby."

The girl reached up, took the phone from my hands, and provided a detailed description, "He's at the Quick Mart on Route

19 West in a brown Chevrolet truck with tinted windows and a Sky County tag that says WILD1. The man is older, with gray hair, wearing a dark green collared shirt and khaki pants. His name is Luther Wilderstein. He's armed."

The dispatcher acknowledged our request assuring us that help was on the way. Trembling like a lost puppy in the rain, the victim handed the phone back to me and found shelter once again under the desk.

"The police are on the way. All of the entrances are secured." I spoke aloud for her sake and to calm my own frayed nerves.

My knee-jerk reaction was to lock the door, but then, a sudden realization halted my steps. "The Two-Adult" rule applies here. At twenty-two years old, I'm barely an adult. I must protect both of us. After all, this is a safe house. I unlocked and opened the door as fast as I locked it, recalling the accountability policy that mandated "two adults are to be present with a minor in a room." I understand the rules. They're meant to increase child safety, protect staff, and reduce our safe house liability.

"I'll stand at the door to keep you safe, but I can't lock it," I was rambling. I stared down the hallway, expecting to see Grace. I prayed fervently, "Dear Lord, where is Grace?" As nerves tightened and tension thickened around me, I knew I needed to steady myself. Despite my training, advocating for a victim on admission was unchartered territory for me. The reality differed greatly from the classroom lectures.

"Grace, where are you?" I blurted out, my words slipping out before I could contain them. Grace has been a guiding light throughout my formative years, serving as both a mentor and a source of wisdom. From her role as my former youth pastor to her current position as a counselor at the Bright Light Safe House, her support has been vital to my own healing journey. Without Grace, I would not be where I am today. She selflessly dedicates her time to this safe house, and I lean heavily on her. I often feel unworthy of her generosity, yet here I am, pleading for more of her guidance.

My gaze fixed on the lock, triggering flashbacks of my own bedroom door ten years ago, as a twelve year old. Back then, that lock was my sole source of protection, offering a semblance of safety as I hid from sight. It became a habit to lock my door, protecting myself from potential danger in the dark of night.

Glancing over at the huddled figure under the desk, mirroring the familiar posture that I once adopted in fear, I felt a sense of determination. Here I stood, a college student with aspirations to aid these young ladies, volunteering at the Bright Light Safe House, juggling incoming calls on the hotline between classes and studying. Typically confined to my office per Bright Light Safe House policy, I wasn't supposed to be here with a new victim, especially a new victim who is possibly being hunted. This was no ordinary admission. This was different. This was serious. Each call we got at the Bright Light Safe House was unique, but this was undoubtedly the most intense case I've encountered so far.

Relieved to see Grace rounding the corner, she walked down the hall holding a crisis admission kit. I purposely introduced them in an attempt to alleviate any doubts in her mind. "This is Grace. She's our lead chaplain and counselor. I'm sorry, I didn't get your name."

She paused for a moment. Her inhale was slow and deep as she hesitated to tell us her name, her real name. My heart ached for her. I could feel the weight of the doubt she was grappling with. It's a battle familiar to abuse victims who have endured a secret life of pain. Standing at a crossroads, torn between burying a harrowed past, they navigate life, experiencing haunting nightmares and unwelcomed flashbacks. Will she choose to disguise her identity, or will she lay down her mask? This young woman can opt for a path of help and healing. However, she knew this route would require laying bare her tainted history and sharing the most shameful and intimate aspects of her life with complete strangers, all while baring her raw emotions. This is precisely why so many victims hesitate to reach out or seek assistance. It's an immense trade-off.

She relented, "My street name is Candy. Please call me by my real name. I'm Hope. My full name is Hope Wilderstein."

With compassion in her sky-blue eyes, Grace reassured her, "It's lovely to meet you, Hope. We're glad you ran to us. We are here to help and support you in any way we can. You are safe within these walls."

Handing her a bag, Grace said, "These are gifts for you."

Grace handed Hope an admissions kit thoughtfully prepared with a warm blanket, a water bottle, some snacks, and toiletries. As Hope received the blanket, she wrapped it around her shoulders as if feeling the collective warmth and care she's missed for so long. Then, seemingly famished, she consumed the water and the trail mix as if she had not eaten in days. Slowly, we could see her body beginning to relax, inch by inch, as the nourishment and care started to take effect.

"Hope, can you tell us how you got here?" inquired Grace.

With shrugged sharp shoulders and her frail hands clasped under her bony chin, Hope recounted the moments before her escape. She knew when they drove past our building that she was going to be free today. As fate would have it, her adopted father and pimp, Luther Wilderstein, pulled into the gas station down the street from our newly opened clinic and shelter, a renovated church. She recognized the steeple lights, the Bright Light Safe House sign, and she remembered our logo, which included a cross, a triangle, and a heart, from our website shared by a friend a few weeks ago.

Explaining in detail, she said, "I knew this might be my only chance to break free from him. Once we pulled into the bay at the gas station, Luther got out of the truck. The gas cap is on the driver's side, so while he turned away to pay for the gas at the pump, I snatched his phone and baseball cap from the front seat of his truck. I pulled the cap down over my forehead, hoping that it would help disguise me. Then, I slid down the seat and carefully opened the passenger door, slithering down to the pavement. I ran as fast I could toward your building."

She paused for a moment to collect her emotions, then continued, "I didn't dare look back. I quickly approached the back door, trusting that someone would answer."

In mid-sentence, the phone rang. My heart raced, and I quaked, breaking the tense atmosphere in the room. It was the police. I answered, hoping for good news.

"Hello, This is Faith–"

"Faith, this is Captain Rhodes from the Sky County Police Department. Thanks to her detailed description, the officers acted swiftly and managed to locate and apprehend Luther within 15 minutes of your call. He was sitting in the truck at the Quick Mart with his window lowered. He was peering through binoculars looking towards the trees behind the gas station. The policeman stated that it was a chilling sight, knowing that Luther was looking for any sign of Hope.

"The policemen pulled in behind him and knocked on his passenger window while another officer snuck up to his driver's side door to close in for the capture. Luther was arrested, handcuffed, and taken to the police station. They found a briefcase with opioids and photos of her inside his truck."

I reassured Hope that Luther, indeed, had been arrested. Exhausted as she processed the news, she laid her head back down into her arms. However, uncertainty lingered in her mind, and she looked up and asked us, "Are you sure they got the right man?"

Understanding the importance of providing closure, we asked the police to bring in proof that Luther was, in fact, the detainee. Just then, two officers entered the room to gather a statement from Hope and to collect Luther's cell phone and cap as evidence. They slowly walked over to Hope, crouched down, keeping a respectful distance while looking her in the eye. They acknowledged Hope's courage in escaping her abuser. With a calm demeanor, my father, Officer Tom Joule, who was a founding supporter of the Bright Light Safe House, showed Hope a photograph of Luther, and without hesitation, Hope confirmed his identity.

"Hope, I have some questions for you. It's imperative that you answer these truthfully so we can hold him in custody. We need your full report as sworn testimony to keep him from hurting anyone else," he told her in a calm manner.

Hope was determined to keep him from ever hurting her again. She told him about when her parents took her in to be their daughter. How she longed for a family and home that provided luxuries and the protection of loving parents, things she never thought could possibly be hers, even in her dreams. But it was all manipulation, a web of deceit Luther skillfully wove around her. Through threats and coercion, he instilled a sense of entrapment within her. She longed to break free but lacked a viable escape plan until her friend introduced her to our website at a recent party. Her intention to seek refuge at our shelter had been brewing, but it wasn't until she spotted our distinctive building that she took the opportunity to run.

With her full permission, we guided Hope to a medical exam room for the intake assessment. Although Hope's verbal statement was dependable, a physical exam with lab confirmation is the most solid evidence permissible in court to secure a long-term punishment for the abuser.

Subsequently, Grace presented her with choices.

"Hope, our program is voluntary. Your future as a restored, recovered woman is possible. Statistics show that those who stay and actively participate in a program like ours return to the outside world with the resources needed for successful healing. Our facilities are safe, and you will be cared for by professionals. You will also be mentored to find a job or go back to school."

"Hope, the next steps are entirely up to you. Since Luther is in custody, the decision is yours. If you choose to stay, we can provide you with meals, a shower, clean clothes, and a bed."

After considering our options, she stayed.

"I'm exhausted. I'll stay tonight. I need a good night's rest," she expressed with relief in her voice.

"Hope, you've made the right choice," I said. "I have to go now but rest assured you are in excellent care with the staff here. Your courage is truly inspiring to all of us. I'll be back at 4pm tomorrow."

As much as I wanted to offer a comforting hug, I understood the protocol not to approach a victim. Tonight is the first night in far too long that her body is her own.

Alone in my car, I breathed a sigh of relief. I checked my phone before I pulled out of the parking lot. My screen showed twelve missed calls and even more missed texts. I looked at the time. My heart raced. I totally forgot about my birthday dinner.

"You're late for your own birthday party. Where are you?"

I texted back, "We had a big save today. On the way."

When I cranked the car, the radio station was playing the six o'clock evening news. The reporter announced the latest statistics on child neglect. "If a child you know needs help, call or text the National Child Abuse Hotline at 1-800-4-A-CHILD or 1-800-422-4453."

The moment these words echoed through my speakers, it felt like a divine sign affirming that our safe house and the people who support it were making a real difference for a population in dire need of our help.

CHAPTER 2

FAITH CELEBRATES

I turned off the radio. Praying aloud, I thanked God, saying, "Dear Father, thank You for Hope's courage. I feel like Hope's safe arrival was a heavenly birthday gift. Thank You, Jesus!"

As I drove over the spillway bridge toward the restaurant, I glanced at Butterfly Lake. My mind played a highlight reel of years gone by. Our journey to help the helpless began exactly ten years before, during our early childhood "Daddy's Angels" treehouse adventures. Dezzie and I would enforce the law and protect our neighborhood, pretending to be undercover police officers. We were on a mission to save lives. Little did we know that those playful beginnings would eventually lead us to confront real criminals.

I pulled into The Crispy Catfish parking lot, where Dezzie stood on the front porch holding a helium "Happy Birthday" balloon. I could see the relief on her face. She took a deep breath and smiled mischievously as she opened the door. As I stepped into the restaurant, a harmony of voices shouted, "Surprise!" There were more family and friends in attendance than I expected. Confetti gradually settled, revealing the beaming faces of my dear friends surrounding the room. With a mix of pent-up emotions overwhelming my soul in that moment, tears of happiness flowed down my cheeks as I gazed upon each friendly face.

I grabbed Daddy's calloused hand for reassurance, looked at him knowingly, and asked, "Is this really for me?"

He beamed and pointed to Dezzie. Dad, still in his police uniform, presented me with a gift. Then, he donned my neck with a huge necklace of dollar bills perfectly creased and folded like flowers around a string. "Mom made it," he said.

Dezzie was the first person to lean in gently as she hugged me and whispered, "Happy birthday. Glad you could finally make it."

I whispered in her ear, "I'm so sorry I'm late. I'll tell you all about it later."

Amidst the whirlwind of school and charity work, finding time to connect deeply with those closest to me proved challenging. I needed this gathering as a chance to reset from today's excitement and remember the blessings of friends and family in my life. Once everyone was warmly greeted, we proceeded to find our seats. Taking my place at the head of the table, Dezzie sat beside me. I looked her in the eyes, and with honest sincerity, grasped her hand and said, "Friends forever, even when I'm late?"

Dezzie has an exceptional talent for offering reassurance even when she needs it too. "Friends forever, even when you're late. I can't wait to hear all about the save," she said with her tan hand on mine.

The drinks were served, and the toasts began. Daddy stood and raised his tin mug of sweet tea, "Can I have everyone's attention, please?"

Once the room was quiet, he started with his usual well-prepared speech, "Welcome, friends and family, to Faith's 23rd Birthday celebration. Without further ado, I want to propose a toast to the birthday girl. Here's to you, Faith."

Dad continued talking after everyone put their cups down, saying, "I want to give a big 'Thank You' to Dezzie for planning tonight's party. She and Faith have been inseparable since before they could talk. As their friendship blossomed, so did their mutual interests. They enjoyed helping our neighborhood as 'Daddy's Angels' when they were younger. And now, they are working as interns at their own nonprofit that helps young girls running from danger. Many of you are already huge supporters of the Bright Light Safe House, and thanks to your generosity, it is now open. Maybe it's not the most uplifting topic to mention at a birthday party, but it is bringing new opportunities to those wounded souls who need help and healing."

Then, turning to look at me, he continued, "Instead of gifts, I have asked everyone to contribute to the Bright Light Safe House. Here's to your mission and charity to others."

Everyone held up their tin mugs in agreement.

I coughed to clear the lump that had formed in my throat and gathered my composure before I continued to speak, "To all of you, I want to begin by apologizing for my tardiness and extend my heartfelt gratitude for waiting patiently. I am humbled to share that all of the contributions donated tonight will be used to further the mission at the Bright Light Safe House. In the seven months since the Bright Light Safe House opened, we have been able to assist over thirty girls. Earlier today, we received a distressed knock at our door. Thanks to the courage of the survivor, she is safe, and her abuser is now in custody."

After a few claps, I continued, "Each rescue is of immense importance, and it marks the long path of healing for these young girls. Their bravery serves as a powerful inspiration, reminding us of the resilience of the human spirit and the significance of standing united in the fight against abuse. I urge you to keep the shelter in your prayers and continue supporting it in any way that you can. Your unwavering dedication is a blessing beyond measure. Each of you here has a special place in my heart. Dezzie and I thank you all very much."

I looked at Dezzie and paused when the emotions swelled inside of me. Thankfully, I saw the waiters walking in our direction, so I decided it was best to conclude my speech. The wait staff, dressed in Riverboat-era style, entered with impeccable timing. The atmosphere into the room immediately transformed to that of a celebration. The cornbread soared gracefully through the air, executing a perfect flip before landing in the sizzling iron skillets held by the skilled waiters.

My gaze shifted to the windows as I caught the reflection of the sunset off the water and the shadows shifting dusky yellow-orange light into the room. This day was truly more than I could have asked for or imagined. Only God knew the events that would fill these last few hours. I quietly thanked Him. With a humble heart and a proud plate full of crunchy catfish, I soaked in each conversation dipped in love.

With balloons flying behind me, candles burning before me, and my loved ones all around me, I smiled. One by one, they got up to hand me an envelope with a card. In each card was money. Dezzie pinned the bills to my shirt.

It was getting late, and the guests were leaving. With full bellies and full hearts, we all walked out together. One more photo and one more "Thank you for coming" until there were just the two of us, Dezzie and me.

I grabbed her arm, interlocking it with mine. "Finally, I can tell you. Get in my car. I have to share with you the most incredible hour that unfolded at the shelter after you left today," I whispered loudly with a hint of excitement.

Recounting the events of Hope's brave escape in vivid detail, from the thunderous knock at the door to her report to the police, my voice got louder and louder. Then, I quietly confessed that I didn't see the missed texts and calls until I got in the car. I apologized again, telling her, "The time raced by, and I completely forgot about my birthday. Dezzie, you'll love Hope. She's strong like us. I'm going to see her as soon as my class is over tomorrow."

Concerned, Dezzie preached safety, saying, "Faith, I'm sincerely thankful you were there to help Hope. But let's consider your own well-being. You could have been hurt. What if Luther had been trailing Hope? What if he made it inside? This isn't our neighborhood mystery-solving anymore. This is real, and this is dangerous. You and I are vital to the hotline desk, and we should focus on handling calls from our small but safe place without ever leaving the office. I truly believe in what we are doing, but we can't sacrifice our own safety in the process. My faithful friend, you have got to be more careful."

I value her pragmatism, truly. However, she's been the caffeine in my morning brew for many years. Dezzie has consistently grounded me in reality, always focused on the task at hand. How should I phrase this? While some label me as carefree, I prefer to see myself as spirited, following the guidance of the Holy Spirit wherever He leads. However, I must admit, there have been occasions when I've mistaken the devil's sly tricks for the right path. She's been the primary witness to my fallacies on many occasions. I knew what she was trying to convey at this moment. What she was really trying to say is that she fears for our lives, and she doesn't want me to get hurt.

I reminded her of our agreement, saying, "Dezzie, remember that more than ten years ago, we made a pact to confront danger head-on while others shy away from it. Our journey thus far has been one of fearlessness, armed with supernatural heavenly strength. We are protected by a force much stronger than any coward or abuser out there. I believe that we should venture into the field more often. Our mere presence can offer comfort to those we help."

She looked at me with disappointed eyes. She placed her hand on mine, sat up straight, and spoke with authority. I knew exactly what she was going to say, but I didn't want to interrupt, so I gave her permission to speak by nodding my head.

"Faith, we aren't children anymore. It's time to use our mature judgment to make wise decisions. We should trust the professionals to do their job while we do ours. I understand your enthusiasm, but we can't let our hearts lead us to believe we're invincible. Caution and vigilance are crucial for the task at hand, without getting carried away by the excitement. We must follow the established steps and adhere to the processes in place," she argued.

Trying to shift gears, I remarked, "Dezzie, with your honesty and unwavering passion for following the rules, you'll undoubtedly make an excellent lawyer one day."

Chuckling, she replied, "And with your adventurous spirit and thirst for excitement, you might just find your calling for the circus."

I smiled. I was relieved to hear her lighten up. She's the constant, steady voice that my sometimes unsteady heart truly needs. Yet, there are days when her cautious demeanor can feel a bit dampening, especially on days when all I want is to be grateful. Her reference to my 'adventurous spirit' and 'thirst for excitement' reminded me of our younger years when we were oblivious to the dangers of the world around us.

"Seriously Dezzie, Hope escaped her abuser and came to us for safety. I had to help her. I wish you could have been there. You would have done the same thing. The more I think about her courage, the more I feel that God orchestrated her timely arrival. Hope is going to join us in this fight. I just know it. She's got a long road of healing ahead of her, but she's one of us," I affirmed.

"Time will tell if she's up to the task. We've lived a lot of life in ten years, Faith. Through the good times and the hard times, we've been a team. I don't want anything to happen to you. After all, we have a lifetime of memories still to make. Please tell me you'll be more careful at the shelter," she steadily urged until she got the response she wanted.

"I promise," I said, looking her in the eyes as I held up my hands in surrender. "I'll be more careful."

It always takes us a few more goodbyes and a few more hugs before we can actually bring ourselves to part ways. The little girl in both of us yearns for just one more day of carefree play as twelve-year-old girls. As I began to walk away, I playfully suggested, "How about a sleepover in the treehouse?"

Amused, she responded, "But it's a school night."

Teasingly I called back, "Party pooper! Well, tomorrow morning, I'll come tap on your window to wake you."

Wistfully, she remarked, "If only we could have one more jump out of the treehouse as Daddy's Angels."

Smiling, I added, "And together, we'd save the world."

She got out of the car, and before she shut the door, she turned and said, "Let's go home."

CHAPTER 3
GRACE COUNSELS HOPE

The next day, I stopped in the Shine Again Resale Store, located just one block up. It's owned by my neighbor, Mrs. West. We met about ten years ago on the first official day on the job as a Daddy's Angel. We were in Dezzie's kitchen when suddenly, Mrs. West knocked at Dezzie's front door. She was searching for her 3-year-old son, Paul. Dezzie and I set out to search for him all over the neighborhood. We eventually found him in the treehouse in Dezzie's backyard. That very day, Mrs. West hired us to watch Paul once a week so she could get some tasks accomplished without worrying about him. Paul was the first child we ever saved from potential danger, and Mrs. West has been one of our most enthusiastic supporters since that day.

"Hello, Faith, how can we assist you today?" Mrs. West inquired.

"We have a new resident at the shelter. I'd like to buy something special for her, something that makes her feel cherished," I explained.

Mrs. West's eyes lit up as if she was seeing her store for the first time. She scanned the racks, showcasing all the items for sale. She slowly danced up and down the aisles, and she told me about a recent donation by an exclusive boutique that she frequents. All of the seasonal leftover clothing that they don't sell, they donate solely to her. Mrs. West is a savvy businesswoman, marketing for us in her free time to local department stores and small businesses. She shares Bright Light Safe House flyers everywhere she goes, telling the story of Dezzie and I finding Paul on the day she thought she lost him forever. She brags about us as if we are her own daughters, the daughters she never had. To hear her tell the story of how we met, you would have thought he was missing for days, but it was only an hour. "A minute is a day for a mom when her child is missing. These girls saved his life," she often says.

Swiping her fingers along the shoulders of a sweater rack, she paused and pulled out a sweater that resembled a luxurious robe. "This sweater is perfect. Look at this beauty," she said as she held up the soft pink duster, complete with pockets and a hood. Mrs. West then slipped it on to demonstrate its charm, striding a few steps up and down the aisle to model its appeal. "She can wear it for any occasion, whether she wants to dress it up or if she wants casual comfort around the shelter. I can't fathom why someone would want to part with this beauty. It's absolutely stunning, and look, it still has the tag on it," Mrs. West exclaimed with admiration. She folded and wrapped the sweater in tissue paper and placed it in a pretty pink bag with a white bow. She always knew how to make these girls feel special.

"Faith, I have a check for you. It's the best one yet. Ever since I started donating ten percent of our sales to the shelter, our business has thrived. Women have been donating large bags of beautiful items. Blessings come in and blessings go out," Mrs. West shared with a warm smile.

"Thank you, Mrs. West. You have always been one of the Bright Light Safe House's most generous supporters."

Driving to the shelter, I had a flashback of the very first day as Daddy's Angels investigators almost ten years ago. On that day so long ago, Mrs. West's knock on the door was reminiscent of Hope's knock yesterday. Paul was lost. She was frantic. The very first day on the job as Daddy's Angels investigators, Dezzie and I found Paul.

I couldn't help but notice the similarity between us finding Paul back then and Hope finding us yesterday. The joy of finding something valuable is like unearthing a cherished treasure. The rush of relief and excitement floods my heart with gratitude and happiness, filling me with a strong sense of completion. It reminds me of hope restored and faith affirmed, leaving me with a deep appreciation for what was lost and found again. I wonder if this is how Jesus feels when a lost soul accepts Him as their savior. I've heard that the angels rejoice in Heaven when a lost soul is found. It's a blessing to share in that joy.

I pulled up to the Bright Light Safe House. I walked straight to Grace's office to find her door open. Grace and Hope were talking. I quietly closed the door behind me and sat in the chair opposite Grace's desk. Between us, on a small table, rested a bowl of chocolates and a box of tissues. I didn't normally meet with clients during their first counseling session, but considering Hope's circumstances, Grace invited me to provide some additional support.

"Hey Hope, I brought you a gift from the consignment shop down the street," I said.

She eagerly unwrapped the sweater and draped it over her shoulders, holding it close and gently rubbing her arms.

"Thank you. It's incredibly soft," she expressed with gratitude. Then, she started to cry. She cried for a long time. Grace and I remained quietly supportive, giving her the space she needed to let her emotions flow. After a moment, she reached for another tissue, took a deep breath, and met our gazes. She tried to talk, but the words couldn't climb up from her heart to her mouth because the tears shoved them down again. After she was able to finally compose herself, she said, "I must have needed that. I haven't cried in so many years that I forgot how good it feels."

"Your tears are welcome here," Grace said.

She admitted between sniffs, "I've become stone cold. I don't laugh either."

Grace encouraged her, saying, "Hope, I'm truly sorry. I haven't been through the same hurt that you have, but I have experienced loss. It's not easy. You're a victim of a crime, and your life will never be the same. We are here to help you grieve, to work through the confusion of it all, and to eventually heal. With good counsel, I believe you can overcome and become stronger."

Hope's somber mood was difficult to encourage. Her defeated posture, with slumped shoulders and frowning lips, didn't show any signs of optimism. "I've kept to myself for so long, I'm not comfortable sharing my life with complete strangers. I know that it seems weird to have trusted you enough to run here, but I just needed to get away from Luther. I don't trust people who are trustworthy. They've always ended up disappointing me. When mom gets here, I'll talk her into moving away where no one knows us. We can start over," Hope confessed.

"Hope, the longer you delay dealing with your problems, the longer it will take to heal. Believe me. This kind of trauma can be pushed down, suppressed to the recesses of your mind, but it won't go away. It has to be wrestled with, chewed up, and spit out. Please do your future self a favor and let us help you. We're in no rush.

Let's just take one day at a time. Job in the Old Testament was a righteous man who lost everything and was deeply distressed. His friends sat with him for two whole weeks before they said a word. We'll be here for you when you're ready to talk," Grace assured her.

It was quiet in the room for a while. We all three just stared at the carpet, occasionally checking our fingernails. I don't know how long to be exact, but long enough to feel the awkward lull.

Grace interrupted the silence. "Hope, we have a small prayer room if you ever want to go in there and talk to Jesus. He's the best counselor, father, and friend. He listens and loves us no matter what we say. He knows you, and He loves you. He'll listen when you're ready to talk."

Hope ignored Grace's comment about the chapel. Her expression changed from sad to mad. My instincts from my own previous experience told me that she was angry at the thought of having to rethink any of her past. Hope looked at me and asked in a sarcastic tone, "Faith, you haven't said a word. What's your deal? Why are you here?"

I recognized that tone. It's one I used to take before I completely healed. In sympathy, I responded gently, saying, "Grace asked me to be here for two reasons. One, I was here when you arrived yesterday, so Grace thought you would be more comfortable with my presence. And second, I'm in school to be a psychologist. I have a passion to help girls like you. Hope, if you are willing, I want to help you heal. I've been through my own healing, and I can attest to the benefits of it. I'm here for you."

Silence fell once again.

"Hope, I don't want to assume what you're thinking, but since you asked why I am here, I want to offer some encouragement. It seems unfair that you would have to do the work when you did nothing wrong. You've been hurt, and you need to grieve. Healing demands a lot from you–more than you feel you have the energy to give. Unloading emotions is exhausting. It may be overwhelming to consider right now, so let's take a break and come back later. While we break, I want to give you something to think about. Here's what I know from my own personal experience and from my research: many women in the world are hurting, and they have never healed. They never forgave their abuser, thinking it would absolve their abuser from consequences. However, it's the complete opposite. The reality is this: Caring for yourself is the most significant step that you can take towards securing your future. If you deny yourself the opportunity to heal, the one who suffers the most is you. Luther and the men who exploited you will continue their lives unaffected. Your anger, tempting as it may be for revenge, ultimately inflicts harm upon yourself," I said.

I drew the words directly from my ongoing research paper, nearly quoting it verbatim.

"How about we take a break and come back in ten minutes," I said. "I've given you a lot to consider."

CHAPTER 4

HOPE ACCEPTS GRACE AND FAITH'S SUPPORT

Grace escorted Hope out to the courtyard where she could walk around the garden and think. The courtyard has been landscaped with a brick path, providing a place to pray or meditate while focusing on their healing journey. It's not a complicated path, but instead, one that keeps them moving forward without having to consider where they're going. This open-air area is located in the middle of our resident's wing and is protected by hedge-lined walls. It's a safe space for these girls to enjoy the fresh air.

Hope walked alone as she thought about our advice. She realized she didn't need to delay her healing journey. Despite feeling physically drained, she harbored a resilience seldom found in girls her age. It's a fortitude born from confronting and surmounting intimate traumas, shaping her into a person of remarkable inner strength. After a short break, I wondered if Hope would come back. Not only did she come back, but she returned to Grace's office ready to talk.

"I don't think either of you would understand my experience." Hope looked down in defeat. Then, after a few seconds, she admitted, "When I passed this Safe House yesterday, I prayed, 'Dear God, please help me!' I can't stop thinking about the push that I got just before I escaped Luther's truck. For the first time in my life, I experienced an overwhelming feeling that I wasn't alone. There was, without a doubt, someone or something that whispered to me that I had to leave immediately or I may die." She took a deep breath, blew her nose, wiped her tears. "I know I didn't escape by myself. I'm thankful for whoever pushed me out of that truck."

Looking at us with determination, she said, "As I ran, I made a promise to God. I told him, 'If I live, if You will give me another chance, then I will do whatever You ask of me.'

I didn't run away yesterday only to keep hiding from the truth. I need help."

"That's what we're here for," Grace reassured her.

"I've never had help. I've always done everything myself, and I'm stronger for it. My biological parents were drug addicts. I don't want to be like them. They couldn't hold jobs; they moved frequently and eventually landed in jail. The foster care system shuffled me from one house to another. While most homes were filled with caring and generous people, I always felt like I didn't quite belong. The families who fostered me often felt obligated to shower me with sympathy when all I truly wanted was to be treated like any other child," Hope shared with a heavy heart.

Grace and I nodded in understanding and leaned forward in anticipation of hearing more of Hope's story.

"When I was ten years old, I was finally adopted. That was six years ago. I felt like I had a real relationship with a mom and a dad - that I was a daughter. In our family, Mom works long hours as a nurse, and Dad works from home. During the week, I spent more time with Dad. On evenings and weekends, Mom and I would catch up on homework, shop, or just hang out watching TV. As hard as he tried, Luther never really knew how to treat me like a daughter. The first few years, I was more like a surprise guest who walked down the stairs each morning. Then, in the seventh grade, something changed. He started to treat me more like a friend. Maybe he felt sorry for me because Mom and I were arguing. She and I could not agree on anything, especially my choice in clothes and makeup. It took time, but I finally started to trust him. He wasn't as concerned about those things, so I started to appreciate his relationship more. He and I didn't argue. Those were good years."

She continued, "Then everything changed about a year ago. With the dip in the economy, money got tight. I could hear them at night discussing the budget and paying bills. I was hoping there was a secret savings account somewhere because I was looking forward to getting a car for my birthday. Dad told me that I would have to save and pay for my own car. We all agreed that we would work a little extra to take the stress off of the family. Mom took a second job as a traveling nurse. I worked part-time at a coffee shop, and Luther trafficked me."

Hope took a deep breath, then continued, saying, "I've never told anyone this." She uncrossed her legs and shifted her weight. Then she leaned forward and clasped her hands in front of her with her elbows on her knees. She began speaking without making eye contact, staring at the ground in shame and regret.

"Dad started to take photos of me." Hope shifted her stare from the ground to Grace and continued, "He told me I could be a model for some of his websites and earn some extra spending money. I didn't realize that he was posting them on a site for men who like young girls. When Mom was out of town for her job, he would sell my photos and pimp me out during school hours."

Hope started to cry again. "I can't go on," she said, sobbing uncontrollably.

Grace encouraged Hope, saying, "Hope, you were born with a natural innocence that sought all that is good, true, and beautiful. Children seek perfection. Your childlike faith was stolen from you at an early age. You may not remember, but there was a time when you possessed innocence. You once lived with a clear, untainted view of the world. It's a sacred space that can never be returned once it's taken, much less stolen. It's a parent's job to protect the innocence of a child. You, Hope, were not given earthly parents to protect you. And for that, I am truly sorry. The good news is that what you have now is a Heavenly Father to protect you. I believe that Jesus was in that truck with you. He gave you that push and held your hand as you ran to us. He can wash all your past away and make you new and innocent again.

Here's what we know for sure: Those who abuse children sexually have the worst kind of addiction. It's different from any other compulsion. Drug addicts abuse their own bodies, so only one body is affected. However, pedophiles and those whose addiction is taking advantage of a helpless child, well, that's an evil like no other. It secretly spreads like a virus, infecting every victim it touches. But there is nothing done in secret that doesn't eventually come to light. You will not be held accountable for the crimes committed against you. But what you do with that hurt from this day forward, that is up to you. I see so much potential for your future, Hope. You are stronger than you think. You can do this. With Jesus by your side, you can."

Hope took a deep breath and proceeded to tell us about Luther, saying, "He had two personalities. One was quiet and kind when Mom was around, and the other treated me like a stranger to be used for his financial benefit when she was out of town. He would call the school, telling them I was sick. He threatened my life if I ever told anyone, especially Mom."

Hope paused, replaying her brave escape in her mind. She put her forehead in her hands. The words slowly dripped off her lips, "Mom is still out of town, so she's going home to an empty house. I've been trying to protect her, but I can't do it anymore."

"Hope, you should call her right now." Grace handed her the phone.

She looked at Grace and said, "You're right, but I can't talk to her, or I may throw up. I'm sick at the thought of the horrible truth. It's easier to pretend it never happened."

Grace asked Hope the hard question, "Hope, what's really holding you back? What are you most afraid will happen?"

Hope knew the answer. Almost as if she was waiting to be asked. She answered immediately, saying, "I've been waiting for a family my whole life."

The tears flowed once again.

"I finally had parents, and now I'm breaking us all up. It's all my fault." She cried, "I'm just not meant to be part of a family." And then, taking a deep inhale and then an exhale, she said with more clarity, "Mom always assumes the best about everyone, especially Luther. She absolutely adores him. I was really hoping that she would find out without me telling her. She may not believe me."

Grace responded with caution, saying, "Hope, I understand your fears. I hear your concern. Your mom may not believe you, but she might. Either way, you are her child, and she has a right to know. We believe you, and we are right here beside you. This is a big step. We will call her and talk on your behalf, but we have to do it today, Hope. We don't need to delay calling your mom. We should have already reached out to her."

Hope dialed her mom's number and gave the phone back to Grace. It rang twice, then three times, and then, there was an answer. Her mom picked up on the other line, "Hello?"

"Hi, my name is Grace. I'm here at the Bright Light Safe House with your daughter, Hope."

"Hand me the phone. I can do this," Hope said as she grabbed the phone from Grace with determination.

"Mom, this is Hope. I have bad news. I'm at a safe house. Luther is in jail."

Hearing her own words out loud caused even more dread within her. A thunderstorm brewed inside Hope. Those sad tears became mad tears, and the cold, unresponsive Hope was colliding with the hot-tempered Hope, causing a twister inside her chest.

"Hope? What did you say? I didn't understand you," her mom said.

She repeated herself, this time shouting out the hard truth, "I'm at a safe house, and Luther is in jail."

"Oh my goodness, Hope. What is going on?" her mom asked.

"Mom, Luther is a monster when you're gone. He's using me to get money so he can pay our bills. He's selling me during school."

Hope's mom was at a complete loss for words, saying nothing.

"You have to believe me, Mom. I don't know how to tell you this, but Luther isn't who you think he is. He's been trafficking me, so I ran away."

"I'm coming home. I'll be there as soon as I can."

"Mom, I'm so sorry, I should have told you, but I was scared. I was afraid for my life."

Listening to Hope apologize to her mom broke my heart. I was getting choked up. But I needed to stay strong for Hope. I tried to swallow it, but I couldn't. The tears welled up in my eyes and spilled over when I blinked. I looked away. All I could think about was the pain and heartache that evil causes families. I grieved for Hope, asking God once again, praying, "Why do so many children have to suffer at the hands of evil people?"

I turned to look at the table behind Grace's desk. Staring at me was a Bible verse. John 10:10: "The thief comes to steal and kill and destroy; I have come that they may have life, and have it to the full."

Jesus's words in black and white printed on a canvas in Grace's office spoke the obvious truth, reminding me that the opposite of all this awful mess is a full life in Christ.

I silently prayed, "Thank You, Lord, for Hope. She is brave with You at her side. Please relieve her of this burden she is carrying."

Hope was still talking, saying, "Mom, please don't worry about me. I want you to come see me when you get back in town, but this is the safest place I can be right now. Mom, I'm right where I need to be. Really, I'm fine."

Uncertain of what to say next, Hope handed Grace the phone.

Grace introduced herself saying "Mrs. Wilderstein, Hope is a brave young woman. I want to reassure you that she is well cared for and secure here at the Bright Light Safe House."

Hope's mom apologized, "I should have seen the signs when she started to withdraw from her friends. She deleted all her social media and stopped communicating with her friends. And then there's her weight loss. Her pants are falling off of her. I just thought she was experiencing typical teenage issues. Our finances were suffering, so I took a job out of town to make more money to support our family. I haven't been there for her when she needed me most. Now, I've lost everything. I don't know what to do."

Grace told her, "Come home."

Hope's mom said, "You're right, I'm coming as fast as I can. Thank you so much for caring for her until I can get there."

"You're welcome. I'll text our address to this number. Call us when you arrive in town."

Grace set the phone on silent, placed it on the desk, and then turned her attention back to Hope.

Concerned, Grace leaned in with her elbows on her knees and asked, "Hope, are you okay?"

She nodded and replied, "Yes, I needed to have that conversation with Mom. She's been in the dark for so long."

Hope's tears rolled down her cheeks heavier than they had yet.

Encouraging Hope like only Grace can, she said, "You did a good job sharing with your mom. It took a lot of courage to tell her what you've experienced."

"I don't feel very strong," Hope's voice cracked as she wiped her tears.

"I imagine you haven't felt strong for most of your life. You've been through so much change in the last sixteen years, but especially in the last two days." Grace kindly gave her a vision for her future, saying, "I want you to hear me say that you, Hope Wilderstein, are an incredibly brave young woman. The strength that I see in you may not be something that you see in yourself yet. It will come in time."

I was still staring at the Bible verse over Grace's desk that contrasts the thief and Jesus. The thief came to steal, but Jesus came to heal. How in the world does anyone abuse a young girl's body? My blood pressure started to rise. Identifying the trigger, I started to remind myself of the best advice Grace has given me. Inhale.

Exhale. Control my breathing. Then I reminded myself of my life's mission: to help these girls who have lost their childlike faith, to heal, and trust Jesus.

Grace explained, "Hope, you have the power of the Holy Spirit over Satan in your heart. Your escape yesterday proves that. We are going to help you listen for the whispers of the Holy Spirit and you'll learn to hear Him and follow His lead, just like you did. We're on the same team, Hope. You can do this."

Grace's words piqued my curiosity and focus, wondering why Grace was so sure that Hope was a born-again Christian, able to overcome with the power of the Holy Spirit.

"Did I miss something? Hope, you're a Christian?" I asked.

Hope responded, "Yes, I am. As of this morning in group therapy, I am."

"Hope, that's good news. Welcome to the family," I announced more excitedly than I should have. The relief that washed over me and the excitement that arose leapt out.

"Faith, I have had a hard life for sixteen years. The last year has been especially dark. I know I need help. If Jesus can help me, I'm willing to try."

Hope was no longer just a new guest at the Bright Light Safe House. She was now my sister in Christ. I immediately started sharing with her as a sister, saying, "Sister, Jesus not only can help you, He can heal you. From the inside out and everywhere in between, Jesus wants to heal you," I encouraged her.

I saw a glimmer of joy in Hope's half-smile for the first time. "And how does that happen?" Hope asked.

"Over time, through prayer, worship, and reading the Bible, God will speak life into you. The earlier you decide to heal, the better."

I gestured to the large mural on the wall behind the couch. It's a painting of a live oak tree holding a treehouse, swings, and silhouettes of girls playing.

"That tree's name is Old Solomon."

Hope turned and looked up at the painting.

"Old Solomon held the original Bright Light Treehouse many years before the Bright Light Safe House. He taught me the importance of approaching healing proactively, much like a tree. Trees have branches that break, but they grow new ones. Did you know that trees heal themselves inside out, using elements that they acquire from other sources?" I looked at Hope and said, "Stick with me. I do have an important point to make."

I pointed to the sun in the painting, saying, "The sun provides the energy trees need to heal themselves, much like God's Son, Jesus. He tells us in the Bible that He is the light that gives us life. In fact, the imagery of light is used two hundred times in the Bible to describe God and his Son, Jesus. They not only give light, but they also give life."

I walked over to the lamp and turned it off and back on to keep Hope's attention, continuing in my efforts to explain, saying, "When we use the light of God as a resource, we heal, and even better, we thrive. If we have Jesus in our lives, we live eternally, forever with Him. If trees don't use their resources to heal, they wither and become frail, eventually succumbing. Similarly, there are people who, like trees, have experienced trauma but never truly heal. They live, but their strength is compromised due to the lack of resources. They seek the wrong chemicals to help them, and so they never find the energy to heal.

Hope, the enemy is going to try to kill, steal, and destroy you by lying to you about your past. He's going to distract you when you try to move forward in healthy thinking. You will have to work hard to overcome the enemy and rise above his temptation to ignore the pain. He's going to tell you that you don't need help. You may struggle to find the energy to go to Jesus with your struggles, but you must overcome that temptation to be alone. Isolation is a dangerous place to be. Don't believe the lies that he will try to feed you. If it helps, claim the name of Jesus. Say it out loud. Jesus loves you, Hope, and He will help you."

"Faith, how do I know Jesus will help me?" Hope asked.

I continued, "Your family branch has been emotionally broken, but I see a new, stronger branch beginning to bud. You're now part of a new family, the family of God. He is your Heavenly Father who loves you unconditionally, regardless of your past. In time, you will grow if you don't give up."

Trying not to overwhelm her, I asked, "Will your mom come to church and counseling with you?" I asked.

"I'm not sure. She told me about how her family attended church every Sunday when she was a child. The church she grew up in was small and more like family. Sometimes, we see those people, and she'll introduce me saying, 'This is Mrs. So-and-So. She practically raised me,' or 'She taught me Sunday School.' She keeps a Bible at her bedside and refers to it often. During my bedtime routine, during the first couple of years that I was adopted, we read the children's Bible before bedtime. As the years went by and I got older, they would tell me, 'Don't forget to read your Bible.' As for counseling, when I became a teenager, if I argued or disobeyed, Mom immediately made an appointment with a counselor. She seemed very comfortable going to that office as if she had been there before. I miss church, and I miss counseling. I trusted the pastor and the counselors. They both seemed very sincere, and I felt more secure when we went. Since she started traveling, we haven't gone to church or to counseling. I think the only reason Luther went was because Mom wanted him to," Hope answered.

"I want you to know that you can trust us and those who work with us. In fact, the officers that came to talk to you about apprehending Luther were actually my fathers, well, my father and my best friend's father. They are some of the best men I know."

Hope asked me, "Faith, you aren't much older than I am, and you're already helping people?"

I nodded and replied, "Yes, I started my healing journey when I was younger. I'll share my story with you another day when we have time. I need to report for my shift in the crisis hotline office. My colleague will be expecting me."

"Faith, I'll go work at the crisis hotline. You stay here with Hope. She might like to hear what you have to say," Grace offered.

I looked at Grace with a hint of hesitancy, "Really?"

"Yes," Grace said with authority. "You can do this, Faith. I believe in you. Just keep the door open."

There, Hope and I sat in Grace's office. I had never shared my story with anyone. I didn't know exactly where in my story I should start, so I went all the way back to twelve years of age, the last year of my innocence. Like Hope said earlier, 'those were the good years.'

CHAPTER 5

THE BRIGHT LIGHT TREEHOUSE

10 Years Earlier:

Dezzie, my closest friend and neighbor, felt more like a sister to me, and her house was like my second home. Firstly, her house was quieter without any brothers around. Although I cherished my brothers, their boisterous teenage energy filled our home. In contrast, Dezzie's family provided a serene atmosphere. Her only sister, Bianca, was born with cystic fibrosis, a condition that causes damage to the lungs and other organs. Consequently, they opted to homeschool due to Bianca's fragile health. Secondly, their backyard sprawled across a larger expanse, offering endless opportunities for our amusement. With its dense foliage and tranquil pond, it transformed into a natural playground where our imaginations could roam freely. Their mom, also their teacher, chef, and caretaker, embodied an aura of peace. Her presence was so comforting, I affectionately referred to her as my "other mother." Their home became a calm retreat amidst the chaos of my bustling household.

Old Solomon, the large live oak tree, lived in the Diamonds' backyard. One evening, Dezzie and I were climbing Old Solomon's branches. "Daddy, can you see me?" We called out to our fathers. Showing off, I climbed up as high as I could into the tree's branches. Our dads, Tom Joule and Tony Diamond, colleagues and best buds, were on the patio supervising the grill.

"Yes, sweetheart, I see you," Dad responded. "Why don't you come back down to the lower branches? I can keep a closer eye on you there." As I made my way back down, my foot slipped, and I struggled to maintain my balance, ultimately slipping and falling onto a lower limb. Thankfully, wise Old Solomon caught me with his broad lower branch, squarely across my back. I drew in a deep breath, followed by a wheezy cough. "Faith, are you alright?" Daddy asked with concern in his voice.

I glanced at Dezzie, sitting just above me on another branch, and I lied. I held up my thumb to let her know that I was going to be alright. Then, knowing that the dads couldn't see us clearly, I grabbed my throat and stuck out my tongue, indicating that I couldn't speak. I was out of breath, my voice temporarily out of order. Dezzie answered on my behalf, saying, "She's alright, just needs a second to catch her breath."

We couldn't afford to give our daddies any reason to abandon the construction of our long-awaited treehouse. We had been eagerly anticipating this project for over eight years.

As we jumped from the lowest branch to the ground, Dezzie turned her back to the dads, and looking at me, she said, "You know, Faith, if you would stop acting like a monkey, our dads would let us have a treehouse."

Still struggling in acute pain but maintaining my composure, I barely responded, whispering, "I know, Dezzie." Holding my back, I said, "It was an accident. Let's swing until supper is ready."

We trusted that our dads could build a treehouse. After all, they partially fulfilled our dreams by installing tree swings. We excitedly witnessed them climb high into Old Solomon, adding heavy extension ropes to his strongest branch. They carefully measured and crafted wooden planks for us to sit on. Securing the strongest holding knots, they secured the seats to the ropes. Watching them take the risk and climbing the greatest heights into Old Solomon's crown only deepened our hope and appreciation for the impending treehouse construction. We trusted that they could build anything we could dream of. We would swing for hours, lost in dreams of our treehouse. Old Solomon's wide-reaching branches extended an open invitation to us every day.

To keep us from grumbling about the long-awaited treehouse, our moms presented us with a challenge: they encouraged us to brainstorm for our future treehouse. They gave us a three-inch binder and told us to fill it with all of our wildest ideas. We scoured library books and conducted online searches, collecting images and inspirations of elaborate houses in trees. Among our favorites was the children's museum treehouse located at an outdoor park on the coast. Suspended off of the ground, it spanned two live oaks, featuring three levels, bridges, and scenic lookouts.

We kept all of our research, designs, and sketches proudly displayed in that binder, and every now and again, we would present its updated content to our daddies. However, we were consistently met with a deferred response, "One day, your dream will become a reality," they would say. "Girls, we aren't going to build the treehouse until you are mature enough to take proper care of it. The answer is not 'no,' but rather, 'not yet.'" With bated breath, we anxiously awaited the day when they would finally declare, "Yes, it's time," to the treehouse we had longed for.

As our hope waned, we prepared ourselves for a heartbreaking "no, not ever" response to our request. After all, we were soon going to be twelve, almost too old to enjoy it. With hesitant persistence, we approached our parents, our shoulders slumped, and an air of doubt surrounding us. We asked, "May we please get a treehouse?"

To our absolute astonishment, they replied, "Yes, it's time. When the weather warms up a bit, we'll build the foundation. Girls, the patience and dedication you displayed while filling that binder with grand treehouses has not gone unnoticed. There's just one more important part of the treehouse to research. While a beautiful exterior matters, should we also consider its longevity? How do you plan to ensure your treehouse will stand without falling?" Daddy asked.

We had not thought about the details of building it from the ground up, as we were hoping our dads would have worked those details out. However, with a newfound spark of hope ignited within us, we were determined to find the answers. Dezzie affirmed, "Faith, we need to call the Children's Museum and interview the builder of their treehouse. If their treehouse can live through storms, then surely ours will too."

Dezzie's mom, Mrs. Moriah Diamond, made a phone call. The children's museum recommended their treehouse expert, Mr. Mike Fields, author of a book and contractor of the construction of treehouses. Mrs. Diamond, always thinking ahead, invited Mr. Fields to lunch. Our hopes of getting our dream treehouse were growing.

The following day, both she and Mom loaded us up in the Suburban for a three-hour road trip to the coast on yet another journey dedicated to our research on our treehouse plans. As we entered the restaurant, we overheard a gentleman talking to the waitress. He was standing at the front by the hostess podium, explaining to her that he was meeting us.

"Mr. Fields?" Mom asked him. "Yes, Mike Fields, nice to meet you. Follow me. I have our table reserved." He walked us over to our table, pulling out the chairs as we sat down. His button-down shirt was tucked tightly into his pleated jeans, and the dirt on his work boots suggested he enjoyed the outdoors. He welcomed us, saying, "What a privilege to meet you. I've heard about your treehouse project. I must tell you how honored I am to share my expertise with you girls."

We ordered a cup of warm gumbo as an appetizer. After the adults made small talk about the weather, he looked at Dezzie and me. "So you like my treehouse at the Children's Museum?"

"Oh yes sir, we do. We really do. We like how you made multiple levels with a lookout tower. The lookout at the top is our favorite part."

"Yes, I made that to resemble the lighthouse on Beach Road."

"Really? I piped up. You won't believe me when I tell you, but our treehouse's name is the Bright Light Treehouse. I never considered adding a lookout tower patterned after a lighthouse, but that would be perfect."

I looked at Dezzie and said, "Don't you think that's a good idea?"

"Brilliant!" she responded.

Mr. Fields, curious to know more, asked, "You're naming the treehouse?"

"Yes, sir. You see, it's more than a place to play. It will be our office. We are detectives and we need a private place to plan our missions."

Mr. Fields looked at our moms. Mom shrugged her shoulders and looked back at us, saying, "These girls are wise beyond their years."

Mr. Fields shook his head, "They are indeed."

Mr. Fields smiled. In my twelve years of life, I've noticed a clear difference between men and women. Men often don't have much to say until someone asks them about their hobbies or work. Then, they have plenty to share. Mr. Fields, for instance, went on and on about treehouses. It's not only his job but also his hobby, so he had double the amount of words for us that day.

He explained, "Girls, the lookout tower will be the last part of the project. The most important part of your treehouse is the planning and preparation. Let's talk about getting started. The success of construction is dependent upon the cornerstone and the foundation." Imparting valuable lessons, he added, "Treehouses don't have a true cornerstone or a foundation, but they do have main supports and a platform for the base that helps hold up the rest of the house."

He reached into his old brown leather satchel and handed us a book that he authored with all of the information he was teaching us. He opened the book and held it up for us to see, saying, "I've illustrated each step for you to get a visual of my explanation. Your first and most critical task is to establish the main supports. Precise measurements are essential to ensure the main supports are perfectly level. Then, the deck will rest on the platform, providing stability so it doesn't wobble. Adding the bracing will hold it steady. Do your fathers like to use tools?"

"My daddy has a tool pouch that he carries around everywhere he goes. He's a policeman, but he knows a lot about construction and fixing stuff. Sometimes, when he's out on a call, he uses his tools to help others." I answered.

Mr. Fields continued, "Good, because he will be drilling a lot of hardware to secure the base and the bracing. Listen carefully, girls," he leaned forward, emphasizing this information, saying, "There is a trick to this step to help your treehouse last that they won't want to forget. If you want your treehouse to last, be sure to add some space away from the tree to allow for growth. Be extra attentive when cutting the hole in your platform for your tree trunk. To save time, this will require some tracing paper or some old newspaper to ensure accuracy. Once again, in this step, as well as with the main support, allow enough space for your tree to grow."

"Got it," I said, drawing an asterisk beside that specific tip in the booklet.

Mr. Fields autographed his treehouse manual, writing in the front cover, "To the dads, Tom and Tony, may your treehouse be evergreen. To the daughters, Faith and Dezzie, may all of your treehouse dreams come true. Best Wishes, Mike Fields"

"I've got to get back to work, but you all are welcome to follow me back to the museum. I'll waive the entrance fee for my newest treehouse fans."

"Mom, do we have time?" Dezzie asked her mother.

"We sure do," she said.

It had been about a year since we had last visited this museum. However, we remembered every exhibit. On the drive over, we planned which exhibits we would go to first, saving Dezzie's favorite, the science experiment room, for last. On arrival, we ran inside to my favorite colossal spiral climbing structure that simulates the sea and spanned the height of the museum. Instead of taking the elevator or the stairs to the second level of the museum, we climbed up three levels to the top. We walked over to the pretend airport and took an imaginary vacation. Then, we dressed up in vintage attire and sipped espresso. Afterward, we shopped at the make-believe grocery store. In the pretend kitchen, we cooked up a fanciful meal. In the art room, we painted Old Solomon and our future treehouse, complete with two swings. Our moms were so impressed that they agreed to frame them and give it to our daddies as an appreciation gift.

Dezzie was a gifted child. Actually, she was smarter than smart. She read science books for pleasure, so in the science room, she explained every scientific law and theory of each exhibit. I became a good listener, shaking my head in agreement, unaware of anything she was saying. She liked to use big words that hurt my brain, but I would just smile and pretend I knew exactly what she was saying. I wondered if all home school children were this informed or if she was the exception to the rule. We explored space and energy, blasting off in a spaceship to orbit and back again. I was drawn back to the learning lab where there was a pulley system complete with ropes and a wheel. I remembered seeing a pulley in one of our treehouse books.

"Dezzie, we need a pulley on our treehouse," I said. "Don't let me forget to ask Mr. Fields about pulleys before we leave today."

I wanted to go back to ask Mr. Fields about pulleys for a treehouse, but I didn't want to stop playing with it as we took turns hoisting ourselves up by pulling the ropes. We spent the entire afternoon playing until closing time. After a long day talking about treehouses, playing in the museum, and outside at the park, we were crazy tired. On the walk back to the car, I couldn't stop thinking about the pulleys. I told Mom that I needed to run back inside and ask Mr. Fields one more question about adding a pulley to our treehouse. The moms were engrossed in a conversation, but I assumed they heard me. Dezzie was reading her new science book from the gift store, but I assumed she heard me too.

I found Mr. Fields, with the satchel on his shoulder, walking out of the museum. He was delighted to tell me about the pulley and rope with a bucket idea. He said, "That might be your favorite part of the whole treehouse. All the details are in the booklet I gave you."

When I returned to the parking lot, my heart sank–they were nowhere in sight. It felt like a surreal nightmare. "What in the world? They left me. Didn't they notice I wasn't in the car?" I murmured aloud as if someone was there to hear my distress.

I ran back to the museum, knocked on the door that was locked, and thankfully the hostess opened the door. "My mom," but unable to conjure an excuse, I simply stated, "She forgot me. Can I use your phone to call her?"

She handed me the phone, and I dialed Mom's number. She answered, "Hello?"

"Mom, this is Faith. Will you please come back to the museum and pick me up? You forgot me," I said.

"Oh my goodness! Moriah, turn around. Faith is still at the museum. Faith, stay right there. We'll be right back."

There I was, waiting all alone. I paced the sidewalk, reminding myself not to let frustration creep in. I scolded myself for not remembering to ask him about the pulley during lunch. I couldn't help but compare myself to Dezzie, who would never have walked away from her mom. "Mom is going to be so mad," I said under my breath. Suddenly, a voice behind me startled me. Mr. Fields called out to me as he was walking out to the parking lot, saying, "Faith, did you forget your mom?"

He brought a smile to my face, alleviating the tension of the moment. I grinned, embarrassed that I was standing there alone. Trying to make light of a heavy situation, I replied, "Yes, I did. I called her to let her know that I got separated, and she's on the drive back to pick me up. They'll be back shortly."

When she drove up, Dezzie and Mom jumped out of the car. Dezzie spoke first, apologizing, "Faith, I'm so sorry. I was so excited about my new book I didn't even notice you weren't there."

Mom hugged me, "Are you okay?"

"Yes, I'm so sorry. I had one more question for Mr. Fields about the pulley, so I went back inside to find him. I thought I mentioned it to all of you, but I guess you didn't hear me."

Mr. Fields, still standing at my side, confirmed that the pulley system would be a good addition to the treehouse. "Yes, the booklet also mentions pulleys and all the optional accessories in the last chapter, starting on page sixty. Please keep in touch with me and let me know how the project is going. It was nice to have met you. Stay safe on the roads."

Hoping to dissolve any tension that remained, I spoke quickly, saying, "Mr. Fields, we will send you an invitation to our dedication ceremony when it's completed. We would love for you to attend."

Dezzie added, "Let's go home." We got in the car.

"Faith," Mom said, her tone measured, "remember the buddy system. Please don't wander off without Dezzie or me. The world can be unpredictable, and I don't know what I would do–" She paused, collecting her thoughts, before adding, "Please, be more cautious."

"You're right, Mom, I'm truly sorry. Thank you for taking us to the coast. Mr. Fields was so friendly," I said.

"I know, right? And he's so smart. He knows everything there is to know about treehouses. Thanks, Mom," Dezzie said.

When we got home, our dads were waiting on us. We told them everything about the day and presented them the instruction manual from Mr. Fields. They were genuinely impressed with our day's accomplishments. To our surprise, they were ready to get started building the treehouse, saying, "We'll head to the lumber yard tomorrow evening to gather all the recommended wood and supplies to start building the treehouse next Saturday."

"May we come along with you?" Dezzie asked. "Faith and I will bring Mr. Fields' manual and check off the list as you shop."

"Great idea, Dezzie," I agreed. We concluded our day with a high five and a secret handshake, sealing our success with a sense of camaraderie. I went to sleep that night dreaming about our treehouse with a lookout tower. Our biggest dream was about to be a reality.

CHAPTER 6

FAITH'S FIRST BREAK

Rising with the sun, as kids often do, I quickly dressed in my play clothes, slipped on my shoes, twisted my long hair up into a big claw clip, and dashed across the street to Dezzie's house. I could see the lamp light peeking out from the cracks in her curtain, so I tapped on her bedroom window on the front right side of the house. Standing under a great magnolia tree decorated with thousands of beautiful white flowers that perfumed the morning air, I heard the choir of mockingbirds who sang from the majestic branches. Nature's instruments were in harmony as I listened to the insects' sharp chords. I snapped my fingers and hummed to the beat of the cicada droning until she opened the curtain and pointed to the front door.

Dezzie opened the front door, inviting me in. "Come on in. Let's go see the treehouse in the morning sunlight." Carefully tiptoeing through the house to the backyard, we skipped across the patio, where we were greeted by our dads. With pride-filled chests and coffee-filled cups held out like a conductor's baton at the end of a beautiful musical, they admired the completed treehouse.

Our dads, not tall men in stature but big in heart, were partners fighting crime full-time and gifted with handy talents on their off days. For the past four weeks, they had committed a large portion of their free time working to bring our treehouse dream to life. Old Solomon held our treehouse. He stood proud on a hill, Mount Moriah, named for Dezzie's mom. Situated perfectly on a lake that reflected the sunrise each morning, it was prettier than we imagined.

Live oaks don't need any accessories to add to their charm, but this amazing tree begged for more attention. In addition to the two tree swings that were already in place, the arms of the tree seemed to hug the deck that held upon its foundation a one-room log cabin-like dwelling with a roof, open windows, and a small opening for an entrance, a perfect fit for Dezzie and myself. Around the outskirts of the treehouse, the balcony spread out on the west side facing the Diamonds' home and hovering five feet above the ground with legs that dug deep into the earth. On the opposite side of the rope ladder, a suspended bridge hung from the balcony to attach to a horizontal branch that held the stairs.

"It's dedication day, girls. Just a few final touches and it's all yours," Dad said proudly.

Mr. Diamond added his compliment, "We are quite a team, Tom. Girls, you bring out the best in us."

The sun's rays cast a warm glow over the shiny, stained wooden planks, and the wind gently rustled the leaves around us. The treehouse stood as a testament to the love and dedication our dads had poured into making this dream come true for us.

The treehouse was not only a sanctuary for Dezzie and me to find peace away from home, but it also served as the official headquarters for our "Daddy's Angels" Department of Investigations. Immersed in our imaginations, we were the epitome of "Charlie's Angels," inspired by the beloved television series that our moms told us about. Just like the characters in the show, we were partners in service to those who needed a helping hand. Given that our dads gave us the assignments, not Charlie from the original TV show, we aptly renamed ourselves "Daddy's Angels."

"It's time to get to work. Faith, you go get your brothers so we can finish up before tonight's dedication ceremony."

Dezzie and I rallied the family to help. While our moms tended to the cooking, the rest of our family joined us in the last-minute preparations. My brothers, Aaron and Oliver, were the muscles that helped lift and move the table, chairs, bookshelf, and a box of supplies up the steps, transforming the inside into a haven uniquely our own. Dezzie's sister, Bianca, and my sister, Joy, with cups of paint and paintbrushes in hand, meticulously inspected the treehouse, making touch-ups where needed. However, my brothers quickly lost their enthusiasm for the task at hand. They would rather playfully wield the tools as swords engaging in imaginative battle rather than use them for their intended purpose. I couldn't help but hear their conversation with Dad earlier as they aired their grievances.

Aaron, my oldest brother, questioned, "How much will we get paid for this?"

Oliver, the younger brother, not one to shy away from voicing his thoughts, added, "Yeah, What's in it for us?"

Dad patiently responded with a pointing finger and head nod towards getting back to work, repeating one of his favorite sayings, "Remember boys, many hands make light work."

"Here, let me help you with that, Tony. Where do you want the trampoline?"

"I'm going to place it under the balcony of the treehouse so they can make a quick exit for their emergency missions," Mr. Tony said.

Dezzie and I gave each other a high five and a secret handshake.

"Who wants to go first?" Dad egged, anticipating our excitement.

I think he was secretly hoping to be the first one to take the leap.

I interjected before anyone else had a chance to respond, "Me please. I want to be first." I climbed up the ladder. My courage diminished with each step.

"This looks higher from up here than it does down there. Dezzie, come on. Let's jump together."

She could see the mixed emotions as a wave of hesitation washed over me. As Dezzie climbed up the ladder, a flicker of uncertainty danced in her eyes. She had initially thought she would jump alongside me to offer support, but as she reached the top, she struggled to find the right words to ease either one of our apprehensions.

"How high is this balcony?" Dezzie asked, knowing the answer but emphasizing her fears.

Her mind raced with thoughts, considering the potential consequences of our plans.

"What if we land at the same time? We'll bounce even higher and maybe even fly off and hit the ground. Or, if we land on one another, that would hurt. Give me a minute to think through this first," she answered her own questions as she evaluated the situation.

As Dezzie continued to calculate the outcomes, my excitement could no longer be contained. I took a leap from the balcony of the treehouse and successfully landed it with a bounce, a celebratory yell, and two thumbs up.

I ran back up the ladder to jump again. "Come on, Dezzie. It's fun. You can do it."

"I'm not ready yet," she said.

"Anyone else want to try?" I asked.

"No. Faith, nobody wants to jump. Let's get back to our jobs so we can jump later." Joy said.

When it came to chores, Joy effortlessly outpaced the rest of us. Joy's firm voice broke in again, "Faith, get down off the balcony and get to work."

I've always admired her and longed for her approval, so I started to turn around and climb down when my brother chimed in agreement.

"Seriously, Faith, stop messing around and get back to work," Aaron echoed.

His comment challenged me. "You're such a copycat. You always repeat what Joy says."

I stuck my tongue out and gave him the scrunchy nose. Daddy swiftly intervened, pointing to his pocket knife. He said, "Faith, put your tongue back in your mouth. The tongue is like a two-edged sword meant to stay in its sheath. I've told you repeatedly not to stick out your tongue. It's not ladylike."

That's when I should have shut my mouth, but curiosity and frustration got the best of me. I couldn't resist asking, "What else can I do when they are being mean to me? Don't I need something to get back at them?"

Dad responded again calmly, "No, Faith, you don't. All you have to do is turn the other cheek."

Despite his wise counsel, I struggled to find the willpower to hold myself back from asserting myself. It was not in my childish nature to surrender to the suggestions of my siblings. Tempted to have the last word, I couldn't resist responding to my daddy's advice. "But Daddy, just one more jump, and then I'll get back to work," I promised.

Determination ran through my veins as I gathered the courage for one more jump. With a burst of energy, I launched from the balcony, executing a flawless backflip mid-air. I felt like an Olympian soaring through the sky. However, as I touched down, Aaron's stout trunk appeared out of nowhere, double-bounced, and catapulted my delicate frame into the air unexpectedly. The sudden propulsion disrupted my balance as I spiraled through the air like a twig in a violent tornado. In a whirlwind of panic and fear, I crashed with my right arm on the metal bar of the trampoline. I let out a piercing scream. Tears rolled down my face as I cried in agony.

"Oh gross," Oliver said as he looked away. "Her arm is crooked, and the bone is sticking out." Dad scooped me up and ran with me to the front yard. My screams echoed through the air to our house, catching the attention of my mom. Mom's complexion retreated to pale, and she almost fainted. Mrs. Diamond's eyes mirrored the gravity of the situation. One of Aaron's friends, Hunt, was driving by. He made a quick stop when he saw us in the front yard.

"Hurry, Get in. I'll take you to the emergency room."

Our moms sprang from the yard to the car to follow us closely as we drove to the hospital.

Much of the drive to the hospital and the emergency room visit is a foggy haze. Somehow, Hunt and Dad got me in the emergency room. I screamed when they examined my arm. Then, the nurse held up the needle. That's the last thing I remember until the nurse returned with a cold rag and smelling salts. She put me on a stretcher and told Mom to sign the consent that read they were going to repair the fractured bones in my right arm. Then, she asked me, "What color cast would you like? We have blue, green, red, black, pink, or white." I was relieved that she said they were actually repairing my arm. I had wild visions of them cutting my arm off completely. "My favorite color is yellow, but since that's not a choice, pink," I responded. Overwhelmed by all of the commotion, I asked, "What exactly are they going to do to me?"

"I'll explain everything to you. The surgery will last about an hour," she said to Mom as she wheeled me away.

The nurse looked over her shoulder and told Mom, "You can wait in here. We'll call this room from recovery when her surgery is completed."

By the time she transferred me to x-ray and then the operating table, the pain in my arm was waking up. However the light beamed over the bed and pierced my eyes. I felt a soft brush sweeping over my arm and up my shoulder as they painted it with betadine and wiped it clean to prepare it for surgery.

They explained, "Faith, we need to take off all of your clothes."

Holding on to my gown tightly with my good arm, I told them as calmly as I could, "Nope. There is no way, not my panties."

I hit a breaking point. Yes, all of this was my fault. No, they weren't taking my panties. Then, I quietly overheard the nurse inform the anesthesiologist of the plan, "Start the intravenous line, and we'll get the panties once she's asleep, then we'll proceed with the catheter insertion."

"You're not taking off my panties."

Those were the last words that came out of my mouth.

The anesthesia knocked me unconscious. In the depths of my sleep, I had a dream. I was sitting alone in the treehouse, gazing at the trunk of old Solomon, the live oak tree. The scars that marred its belly, remnants of long removed branches, took on an appearance that I never noticed before. The scars were a semblance of a misshapen face. The round, uneven eyes stared at me. The partial nose was off to one side, and two jagged lines resembling lips moved. I looked away, thinking that I was hallucinating.

When I looked back at the tree, the features came to life. The uneven eyes opened, and the mouth twisted into a menacing grin as it taunted me. The voice that emanated from the unsettling visage was deep and low.

"Faith, your impulsiveness is straining your relationships. Engaging in conflicts with your brothers and disregarding the thoughtful advice of your sister and friend is imprudent. While a broken arm is unfortunate, it could have been far more severe. Consider the consequences of your carelessness. You wouldn't want to lose your arm. Think of me. My branches were pruned, and I sprouted new ones. You can't grow more arms. This is the consequence of your unwise actions. Reflect on the day and the mess that has unfolded. A promising day has been tarnished."

These words clashed in my mind as he pressed on, "Faith, you and Dezzie refer to yourselves as Daddy's Angels. Angels are warriors for the Lord. They don't get promoted to help God from falling and breaking their wings. They rise in rank as they are obedient and serve Him wholeheartedly. I'm not saying that you and Dezzie should change your name, but perhaps you should strive to live up to it."

He wasn't happy. Perhaps he's angry we didn't ask him permission to put the treehouse in his branches? He's not the only one that's disappointed in me. Old Solomon's words held undeniable truth.

"Faith," Old Solomon repeated my name, trying to get me to respond. I heard it again. "Faith, wake up. Surgery is over. You're in the recovery room. It's almost time to go home," the nurse informed me.

As I gradually regained consciousness and lifted my heavy eyelids, a wave of relief washed over me as my family appeared through the sleepy fog. Around my hospital bed, I saw double of my mom's face. Caught in the throes of double vision and delirium, my mind was playing tricks on me. With an exuberant giggle, I realized my distressing dream wasn't a reality, and I exclaimed, "There are two of you."

Mom quipped, "I wish there were two of me."

As her face finally came into focus, I asked, "How long was I asleep?"

Mom answered, staring at my cast that started at my hand and covered my arm all the way up to my shoulder, saying, "It's been two long hours."

"What time is it?" I pressed, wondering if the day was over. Then, tearing up, I asked, "Did I miss the treehouse dedication?"

To my relief, she reassured me that it was still light outside. "Oh Mom, I'm sorry. I shouldn't have jumped from the treehouse."

My heart went out to Aaron, considering how frequently he found himself in trouble. I imagined that once they returned home the work proceeded swiftly to avoid the release of Dad's anger. He had a knack for turning incredibly quiet when he was upset, and I could envision them diligently working without exchanging a single word.

When they wheeled me into the Same Day surgery room for discharge, all the family was there, including Dezzie. Aaron stepped forward, his remorse evident in his voice as he apologized, "Faith, will you please forgive me for bouncing you and causing you to fall?"

With sleepy, slurred speech, I responded, "You are forgiven."

Hunt, Aaron's friend who drove me to the hospital, was standing beside Aaron, so I thanked him for driving me to the hospital.

"Oh, I was happy to help you, Faith. You're like a little sister to me anyway. I went back to help with the treehouse. It's really nice. Maybe just use the stairs to exit next time."

Joy, my sweet sister, always the peacemaker, spoke up, "The Bright Light Treehouse is complete. The freshly painted trim is drying as we speak." Bianca stood beside her, held up her hands, and pointed at her shirt splattered with paint, saying, "Yes, I have proof."

Then Oliver spoke up, "The furniture is set up just like you drew on the plans."

Dezzie couldn't contain her enthusiasm. "The sign is all that is left to be hung above the door. Everything else is in place. Trust me, Faith, you're going to love it."

It seemed as if my broken arm served as a catalyst to cause them to work even harder.

Then, they all said at the same time, "NO JUMPING."

I pulled up the covers and reached down with my left hand as I remembered my panties. The nurse held them up in a bag and asked, "Are you ready to get dressed?"

They all laughed while I blushed with embarrassment.

Before everyone left the room, I asked Dad and Dezzie to stay. I thought about the disturbing dream of Old Solomon and his gnarly face that spoke to me. Remembering the tree's disparaging words, I knew I owed them an individual apology.

I addressed Dezzie first, apologizing, "Every time I try to prove your fears wrong, I only prove them right. I don't want you to be such a scaredy-cat. I want to show you how to be brave." Looking down and then back at her, I confessed, "I messed up. Will you forgive me?"

"Yes, I forgive you," she said.

"Daddy, you and Mr. Diamond poured your hearts out to make this dream come true for us. You were as excited about this day as we were. I'm truly sorry that I ended up causing a mess," I lamented.

With an understanding smile, he said, "Faith, all those years you begged me for a treehouse, and I said, 'No, not yet, it's not time.' You thought I was being mean. A good father does not give his children gifts that are dangerous. Do you know why?"

I responded with guilty tears, "I wasn't ready?"

"Faith, I know you better than you know yourself. As your father, it is my responsibility to protect you. Now you are twelve. It is your role to take accountability for your actions. Yes, I forgive you, Faith."

Dezzie approached me, gave me a gentle hug on my left side, and said, "Let's go home."

"That's it! 'Let's go home.' Dezzie, that's your code sentence to remind me to stop and think about my actions. I knew you would think of something brilliant," I acknowledged.

I stared at the pink cast that covered my right arm the whole drive home, remembering Dad's proverb, "Obedience gets the blessing, disobedience gets the punishment."

It was a cool evening at sunset as family and neighbors circled around the front of the treehouse in the Diamond's backyard. With the sunset over the horizon, string lights hanging in the tree, and tiki lamps lining the path from the patio to the treehouse, the mood was set for a party. Mr. Diamond hammered in the nail directly over the middle of the door frame and hung the sign with a cross, a triangle, and a heart. The words were engraved above each symbol, "Jesus changes hearts."

Then, he commenced the treehouse dedication speech, "Today we dedicate this treehouse to be the official headquarters for the

Daddy's Angels. Since Dezzie and Faith have recently accepted Jesus into their hearts, they wanted their logo and mission to state, 'Jesus changes hearts.' May your heart lead you to pure actions."

Dad appeared from behind him, brought out a box wrapped with a bow, and said kindly, "Faith and Dezzie, this treehouse has been a big dream of ours for a long time. Today, it has become a reality. I have a surprise gift for you."

Dezzie and I tore the wrapping paper and opened the heavy box. There was another sign that read, "The Bright Light Treehouse: Daddy's Angels Headquarters, Det. Faith Joule and Det. Dezzie Diamond"

"I absolutely love it. Thank you, Daddy and Mr. Diamond," I exclaimed joyfully. "It's official. We're in business."

And so, the treehouse became not only a physical space but a symbol of love and the bond between us and our dads. Mom captured a photo of Dezzie and me proudly holding the new sign.

"Smile and say cheese!"

CHAPTER 7

DADDY'S ANGELS

Dezzie pondered her options for an after-school snack, "Should I go for peanut butter and jelly mixed in a cup or pimento cheese?"

"I love you, friend, but I totally don't get your snack choices." I made myself at home, retrieving the carrots and Italian dressing out of the fridge. With my one good arm, I ate while we planned our evening.

She settled on the pimento cheese. After shoving a heaping tablespoon in her mouth, she sat back in the chair, swallowed, and said with her eyes closed, "That is so satisfying."

I scrunched up my nose and shivered at the thought. "Yuck!"

"Let's talk about something we can agree on. Our first Daddy's Angels ad will be featured in the next email to the neighborhood. We'll include a photo of the treehouse along with an announcement about our mission, our job descriptions, contact information, and hours of operation," Dezzie announced with authority.

Mrs. Diamond asked me, "Faith, do you like this photo with or without your daddies?"

"One hundred percent with them."

Dezzie agreed, "I like that one too. Now for the heading, 'Daddy's Angels: Neighborhood Girls on Mission to Help You.'"

We meticulously planned every detail of the ad. Mrs. Diamond, ever supportive, typed it up for our approval. She signed the email, Moriah Diamond, President of Forest Glen Homeowners Association. With a click of a button, we would be official. She clicked on the word "send."

"There it went, girls. The neighbors will be reading the HOA email complete with your Daddy's Angels advertisement attached." Mrs. Diamond was our acting secretary, helping us market our community service aimed at a spirit of loving our neighbors as ourselves. She also included our credentials: "Calling all Neighbors, let our sixth-grade girls, capable of performing light responsibilities, help you today."

"I can't believe this is happening. It's finally real," I said. "We're a great team."

"Girls," she counseled us. "Not everyone is going to need help, but for the ones that do reach out, always be kind. Be a cheerful giver of your time and abilities. Always stay together. You two are a great team when you remember the rules. Don't forget the buddy system. After all, even your dads are partners. As trained policemen, they go everywhere together." She could see that we were not paying full attention when she spoke up. "Are you listening? This is important. Most of our neighbors are friendly, but for safety's sake, always get my approval before you go to anyone's home," she commanded.

Suddenly, there was a knock at their front door. Then, the doorbell rang. Their next-door neighbor, Mrs. West, continued to knock on the door with rapid-fire tapping until we answered it.

"Have you seen my son, Paul? He's only two. I can't find him."

"Have you sent out a neighborhood email alert?" Mrs. Diamond asked as she refreshed her screen.

"No, I need help. Should I call the police or keep knocking on doors? I don't know what to do. He's never walked off before."

"Mrs. West, please excuse me for interrupting, but Dezzie and I will find Paul. You stay here with Mrs. Diamond and call the police while we check with the neighbors. Come on Dezzie. Let's go."

We asked every neighbor on our street and on our block. No one had seen little Paul. We returned to Dezzie's house and asked Mrs. West if they heard from the police.

"No, girls, we haven't. Keep looking," Mrs. Diamond told us.

"Daddy put extra maps of our neighborhood and walkie-talkies on the shelf in the treehouse. Let's get those."

"Good idea!"

We sprinted out the back door, across the bridge and up the steps. As we approached the entrance of the treehouse, there was a thump on the floor of the treehouse. It sounded like a beat of a drum.

"Shhhh! Did you hear that?" Dezzie asked me.

"Hear what?" I asked, hoping that I didn't hear what she heard because it scared me. I preferred to ignore it in hopes that it would go away. I looked up in Old Solomon's branches, thinking a small branch fell. Then, I heard a rip and crinkle of paper. I crouched down outside the entrance and signaled for Dezzie to get down behind me.

I put my index finger up to my lips and whispered to Dezzie, "I heard something. Get behind me and get ready to run. It may be a rat."

"What if it's a raccoon or a possum?" Dezzie asked.

I repeated the plan, "Get ready to run, Dezzie."

I hesitated to look. Then, I remembered our pact as Daddy's Angels "to confront danger head-on and not to shy away from it." I carefully peeked my head in.

To our complete surprise, there was no small creature, but there was a cute red headed little boy sitting at the table eating from a snack-size bag of chips.

Approaching the boy slowly so I didn't scare him, I bent down and asked, "What's your name?" I asked.

With a mouth full of chips, he answered, "Paul."

I turned and spoke slowly, "Dezzie, you stay here. I'll go get his mom." I ran back down the steps and across the rope bridge to Dezzie's house.

Walking in the door, I yelled out, "Mrs. West, we found Paul!"

She came running to me. "Where?"

"He's in the treehouse. Come look," I said, grabbing her hand.

"Paul, I'm so glad you're okay!" She cried and hugged him for a long time. "I should have known to look here first. All he has said over the last few days is 'treehouse, Mommy, treehouse.' We were here for your dedication ceremony last weekend, and he enjoyed climbing up the stairs and touring the treehouse. He didn't want to get off of the swing, so I promised him that we would come back to play. This makes complete sense now. Hindsight is always twenty-twenty."

"Mrs. West, what does that mean? Hindsight is twenty-twenty?"

"It means that reflecting on the past should have given me a perfect view of the current situation," she explained.

"I get that. I completely understand. I felt that way after I broke my arm. Yes, hindsight is certainly twenty-twenty."

"May I make a suggestion? Paul could come over once a week to play in the treehouse with you girls while Mrs. West gets some housework done," Mrs. Diamond said.

"That's a great idea, Mom. We need babysitting jobs. Mrs. West, If it makes you feel better, we're licensed babysitters. We took a babysitting class, including CPR, last year at the Baptist Hospital," Dezzie said.

We heard a police car drive up with a siren. Dad got out, "Hey girls, We are working a 'missing child' case in our neighborhood. You girls want to help?"

"Guess what?" I said as I held Paul up in my arms like a trophy. "We found him in the treehouse," I reported.

"Wow!" He looked at us with wide eyes, searching for the right words to say. "Well done, girls. You're natural investigators."

"Oh it's nothing, Dad. He made it easy for us. We were going to fetch the maps and the two-way radios when, all of a sudden, we heard something. We actually thought it might be an animal of some kind. To our complete surprise, it was Paul."

"I know Mrs. West must be grateful for you both."

"Yes, since little Paul likes the treehouse so much, she's going to bring Paul over to play once a week so we can watch him while she goes out."

"See? One job well done leads to another. In fact, since you have time, I have another assignment for you. Another neighbor needs your help. The Boutwell family's dog has had puppies, and she's been missing since lunch. Those puppies are starving. Here are some signs. Grab a hammer and nails out of the toolbox and post one sign on each street light pole on the street corners in our neighborhood. Stick together. Watch for the cars. Look both ways before you cross the street. And remember, I don't ever want you girls wandering off alone."

"Sure, Dad. You can count on us."

"This is fun," Dezzie said. "But I do have a lot of homework. Let's get this done and get back before dark so we can eat and study."

"Hello, it's Friday! We can do homework tomorrow."

I held the extra signs with my left hand while she hammered them one by one to each light pole. I wasn't much help with my broken arm. Up and down the streets of our neighborhood, we ran.

Mr. O'Conner stopped his truck and asked us, "Hey girls, what's on your sign?"

"It says, 'Lost Dog.' She's a mommy dog, and her puppies are at home starving."

"I'll keep an eye out for her. For your safety and consideration, you should know there's wild animals that roam in the woods at the end of my cul-de-sac on Forest Glen Circle. You girls don't walk back there. Let's wait and see if anyone responds to your signs. If they don't, I'll search back there in those woods. Give me a few of those signs. I'll be happy to post some of those on my drive home. That will save you a little time."

"Thank you so much," I said and handed him a few flyers and nails.

Thinking out loud, Mr. O'Conner considered where the mama dog might be. "I sure hope a cougar or a bear didn't get her. In fact, did you girls know that, in addition to the animals that we see, like the white-tailed deer, there are several species that we don't see unless we go deep into the forest? Some are better at camouflaging themselves, and they are sly like the foxes. There are very few sightings, but in the past, there have been wild hogs, bobcats, and even bears.

Dezzie's spirit of curiosity started with the questions, asking, "A bobcat? Have you ever seen one?"

"Yes, I have. I've seen a few over the years. I work for the Forestry Commission, and we care for the trees in our state. I help landowners protect their trees from pests. We manage these animals by conducting forest pest surveys. Animals get very protective when they have babies. If that mama dog considered any of those animals a threat, she may have chased them down. You girls be careful."

"Yes, sir, Mr. O'Conner. You've got me thinking about my own backyard. Can I ask you a big favor? I live at 312 Wild Flower Way. Will you come by my house and inspect our trees for pests?" Dezzie asked. "We have a treehouse in an old oak tree, and I want to be sure there are no pests in my yard that will hurt our tree," Dezzie inquired.

"Good idea." I patted her on the back.

"Sure girls, I'll be there tomorrow evening about this time. I have to go home now. Mrs. O'Conner is expecting me."

"Did you hear what he said? We have to go back there in those woods to find the mommy dog. That's where she is," I prodded.

"Faith, stay focused. We need to finish this job and get home for supper. What would our daddies say if they found out that we were exploring the woods without them? If a sixty-five pound Lab can be taken by one of those beasts, don't you think they could easily enjoy our 90 pounds for dinner?"

"My brothers and I go into those woods to fish in the creek. I've never seen any animals. I'll ask Oliver to take us. Our dads won't care," I said.

Dezzie shook her head in disappointment. Her parents never allowed her to walk around the neighborhood without an adult, much less go into the woods.

"The only reason my parents are letting me go out this afternoon is because they know we have a mission to accomplish and that we'll be back before supper. We only have a few more signs to post. Let's knock this out. I'm getting tired."

I said one more time, just in case she changed her mind, "Come on, you know it would be cool to see a real live bobcat. We could just watch it from a distance."

Dezzie remembered the new code phrase we agreed to use when I get ambitious. Reminding me nicely, she said, "Let's go home."

I responded with regret. "You're right," I admitted. "Let's go home."

We walked in the house to see Mrs. Diamond stirring the peas.

"Girls, you're right on time. Wash your hands and set the table. Supper is ready."

"Mrs. Diamond, you make the best crowder peas on the planet. After all that walking, I'm going to need extra," I said.

"You can have a whole plateful if you want."

"Has anyone else seen our ad or emailed back for help?" Dezzie asked.

"Yes, within minutes, Mrs. West was responding to the email. She shared how quickly you offered to help her find little Paul. She complimented you both and highly recommended you to the neighborhood. Any luck finding the Mama Lab?"

"We did get all the flyers posted, and we met Mr. O'Conner. He mentioned the wild animals in the woods beyond his cul-de-sac. Mr. O'Conner has a theory about that mama dog. He suggested that the wild animals in the woods may have attacked her."

"You girls will not go into those woods without your daddies. Understood?"

"Yes ma'am. I was afraid you would say that," I sadly responded.

Dezzie flashed her eyes at me and raised her eyebrows. She quickly changed the subject, saying, "Mom, did you know that Mr. O'Conner is a professional with the Forestry Commission and knows all about trees and wild animals? He's coming over tomorrow evening to look at Old Solomon and examine him for any pests. We want him to see the treehouse to make sure it's safe."

"Speaking of safety, I can't help but wonder what those poor puppies will do without their mother tonight?" I said.

"The Boutwell family will need to feed the puppies a bottle, just like human babies," Mrs. Diamond answered.

"Oh, how cool. Can we help feed them?" I asked.

"That's a good idea. Puppies eat a lot and eat often. I'll let her know that you girls are willing to help them by taking an afternoon feeding until they find the mama."

Mrs. Diamond's phone rang. "Hello, this is Moriah."

It was Mrs. Boutwell. She thanked us for posting the "lost dog" signs. She also accepted our offer to feed the puppies tomorrow afternoon.

"Girls, your first day as Daddy's Angels has been a success. You've completed today's missions, and you have two jobs as a result of your great work, babysitting and feeding puppies. Who wants to celebrate with chocolate chip cookies and milk?"

"Yes, please," we sang in unison.

Dezzie poured the milk in a wide-mouth mug, perfect for dipping our cookies. I don't know if it was the sugar or the day's excitement, but we rattled on and on about our day one more time, making sure we didn't miss anything. We laughed until tears rolled down our cheeks as we remembered the looks on our faces when we heard the thud and the crinkle of the paper in the treehouse. "You almost peed in your pants, Faith Joule!" Dezzie said.

"Ha! I was the one in front who was protecting you. Who knows? It could have been a black bear. I hope those wild animals stay in Mr. O'Conner's cul-de-sac where they belong."

"What would we have done if that was a raccoon instead of a little boy?" Dezzie teased.

"I guess we would have seen how fast we can run," I laughed. "Oh, me. As much as I want to stay, I really should get home. Thank you, Mrs. Diamond, for all of your help today. I think this Daddy's Angels idea you gave us is going to be a huge success."

CHAPTER 8

THE MIRACLE OF LIFE AND LIGHT

The next morning, I walked outside to check the weather. The sun was shining, and the air was warm. Dad was outside working on the car with his radio blasting the name of the station, "The Best of the Eighties and Today."

"What's the high today, dad?" I asked.

"It's going to be warm like my favorite decade of music-in the eighties." He winked at me. He was a little corny sometimes, but I sure loved him. "Hey Faith, I'm proud of you and Dezzie for finding Paul and posting those signs yesterday. Before you two get busy with detective work today, don't forget your priorities around here. Check with your mom to be sure she doesn't have any chores for you first."

"Yes, sir," I said. "Have you signed me up for softball yet?"

"Yes, in fact, Tony and I have volunteered to coach you girls. It's the first year for stealing bases. I bought you a Slip 'N Slide at the store. You should take it over to the Diamonds and practice with the new neighbor. Georgia is her name. She's older than you girls, but she's the best on her team. I bet she'll show you how."

I packed a duffle bag with a Slip 'N Slide, a towel, and my bathing suit. Dezzie and I would have some time to practice our sliding this morning before we fed the puppies. I picked up the bag with my left hand and walked across the street. Mr. Diamond was on his way out the door to go help Dad with the car. "Good morning, Faith."

"Good morning; is Dezzie up yet?"

"Yes, she's finishing breakfast. Can I help you with your bag? That looks like a lot to carry with one arm," he offered.

The sun warmed me as a cool breeze blew. It was the first Saturday morning of spring in March.

I walked to the kitchen where Dezzie was washing her dishes, "Hey Faith, what's in the bag?"

"I brought my bathing suit and a Slip 'N Slide. We need to practice our sliding techniques for summer softball," I offered.

"Faith, you shouldn't slide until your arm is healed. Remember what your doctor said: 'No sports, no gymnastics.'"

"I'll be fine. Sliding is not a sport, nor is it gymnastics. Will you put this bread sack over my cast and wrap it tight with this zip tie? I can't get it wet."

We hooked up the water hose to the slide. Our new neighbor, Georgia, who was two grades older than we were, was outside on her swing set.

"Hey Georgia, would you like to come over and practice sliding with us? You can give us some of your best tips," I said.

"Sure, I'll be there in ten minutes."

After she walked in her house, I told Dezzie, "My daddy said she is an awesome softball player and has the best batting average on her team. That means she gets on base and runs home almost every time she gets up to bat. I'm going to ask her to help us with our hitting techniques after we slide."

"How will you swing a bat? With one arm?"

"Exactly," I said, "no problem."

Georgia came through the side gate, wasting no time to give us her best tips. "Alright girls, first, we're going to learn how to slide. Rule number one: Never slide into first base," Georgia coached us. She gave us sliding instructions, starting with the head first, "Faith, you should stand back and just watch this round."

They started at the top of the hill, running as fast as they could, one at a time, down to the Slip 'N Slide, diving head first with their arms stretched out. I stood at the end, watching and pretending to be the umpire. Squatting down to see their hands meet the end of the Slip 'N Slide, I spread my left eagle arm out, raising my right elbow in the sling, and yelled, "You're safe!"

Then, I joined in as we practiced sliding feet first. Georgia took great pride in teaching us everything she knew, saying, "Sliding is a game changer. You'll definitely help your team win if you don't mind getting dirty and if you can handle a little pain."

She showed us the bruises on the side of her hips from her team practices. "That looks like it really hurts," I said.

"No pain, no gain, girls. It only hurts for a little while," Georgia said as she wiped the grass off of her leg.

I noted, "Georgia, you glide down the slide so much faster than we do. I hope I'm as fast as you are one day."

"Faith, Georgia is faster than us because she's bigger," Dezzie responded before she thought about her words.

Georgia stood back and puffed her chest out.

"Are you calling me fat?" she asked, popping her knuckles as if she were preparing her hands for a fight.

Dezzie quickly explained, saying, "No, not at all. Let me rephrase that. You're taller and older than us. Basic physics will tell you that the speed of our movement depends on the mass and force. Georgia, you are taller and stronger than us, so therefore, you move faster than us. It's a compliment, not a criticism. Do you girls not remember those Laws of Motion? One of the laws states, 'Force equals mass times acceleration.' In Other words, a taller girl is going to slip and slide quicker down a hill than a smaller girl. We learned this in science using different size balls rolling down a hill." Dezzie twirled around on one foot like a ballerina with her fingers stretched out and said, "I love science."

Attempting to divert our attention from science to something more interesting, I said, "Georgia, we are going to help feed some puppies later with a baby bottle. There's nine of them. Do you want to go with us? We could feed three each. I'm not as smart as Dezzie, but I know basic math."

"Sure, that sounds fun. What happened to the mama dog?" Georgia asked.

"She is missing. We posted signs last night in hopes that someone would find her," Dezzie answered.

"Do you know who the daddy dog is? Maybe she went to visit him," Georgia offered.

"I never thought of that. Good question. We'll ask Mrs. Boutwell."

"Do you know how dogs make babies?" Georgia asked.

Proud that I knew the answer, I responded, "That's an easy question. God creates them, and then He blesses the mom with babies in her tummy. She has them within a month or two. All babies are a miracle, even puppies."

"Yep, that's how it happens. Babies are a gift from God in Heaven above. Mom says that all the time," Dezzie confirmed it.

Georgia laughed, "Have a seat, girls. It's my turn to teach you a little something about science."

She told us everything we didn't know and some things we didn't want to find out. After she taught us how babies are made, my left hand instinctively moved to cover my shocked expression. I couldn't believe what I was hearing. Glancing at Dezzie, I saw that she, too, was clearly in shock. Her face turned a few shades of pink, and her expression froze with her mouth open as though she had just seen a ghost. I could only imagine all of the questions racing through her mind.

Georgia looked at us and whispered, "You can't tell your parents that I told you, or they won't let me hang out over here. If you have any questions, feel free to ask me or my parents. They know all about it. My dad is a baby doctor, and my mom works in his office. I'm sure your parents will tell you all of this soon enough. I hope you appreciate me when they do tell you, so you won't be as surprised as I was. Seriously, I'm actually doing you a favor. You're going to be teenagers soon, and you'll be going through some changes from head to toe. There's a lot that will happen to your body to prepare it for childbirth. You know, some say Mary was thirteen when she had Jesus."

"Yes, and Mary was 'with child' by the Holy Spirit. That's why they call it an immaculate conception," I responded, feeling some-what relieved that she brought up Jesus' birth in our conversation. It made me think about the Christmas story. That was going to be one of my first questions to Mom.

"Yes, and that's why it's considered such a miracle of God. It wasn't the normal way that babies are usually conceived," she argued.

Dezzie's mom whistled and called out for us, "Girls, the Boutwell Family is ready for you. Can you be there in thirty minutes for them to show you how to feed the puppies?"

"Yes ma'am, We'll be right there," I hollered back.

This conversation about babies opened up a flood of questions in my mind, and I was desperate for answers. "Georgia, would you please come with us to feed the puppies?" I looked her square in the eye, "Please, be honest. Did you make all that up?"

"I just remembered something," Dezzie interjected, her voice breaking her unusually long silence that lingered since Georgia sat us down for the uncomfortable science lesson. "I had a biology lab in my science co-op last year with flowers. We talked about the male stamen and the female pistil. Those were called 'the reproductive parts of the flower.' Every living organism possesses a means of reproduction. We've learned about the differences between mammals and reptiles, genes, and traits. Interestingly enough, no one has shared with us the topic of human reproduction."

"Can you imagine learning this in class at my school? I wouldn't be able to look a boy in the eyes all day long or perhaps the rest of my life. I don't think I'll ever get married," I said.

"Faith, God created all things, people and science. When Mom teaches Bianca and me about science, she always ends her lesson with a Bible verse from Psalms that says, 'You are fearfully and wonderfully made.' Now I know what she's talking about. I don't know about the 'wonderfully,' but I understand the fearful part. I'll ask Mom about this later. But for now, we have puppies to feed."

The Boutwells' house was only one block over. The hungry puppies looked like round balls of fur snug in their crate. Some were black, some were brown, and one was silver. She gave us a quick lesson on how to hold them, feed them, and carefully place them back down. We each picked up one of the hungry puppies, fed them the bottle, and then placed them in a separate crate.

After feeding three puppies each, we each wanted to keep one for ourselves.

"We'll be happy to help with these little hams anytime," I offered.

Mrs. Boutwell complimented us, "Girls, you're all good substitute puppy moms."

"Will you be keeping all of these puppies?" I asked.

"We'll sell all but one of them. This silver one is for me."

Dezzie, Georgia, and I all said at the same time, "I want one."

"Ask your parents. Puppies are a lot of responsibility. And from the email I read, the Daddy's Angels are going to be very busy. You girls keep your eyes out for Bonnie, the mama Lab. She's out there somewhere. Until she finds her way back home, you girls can feed these hungry hams anytime. Come back and see me tomorrow after church, and we'll talk about the responsibilities of owning a puppy."

On the walk home, we talked about names and even planned puppy play dates. Then Dezzie remembered, "We have to hurry back. I almost forgot about Mr. O'Conner's appointment to look at Old Solomon for pests."

"Bye, Georgia, we'll see you tomorrow," we said as we went our separate ways.

Mr. O'Conner was right on time. Just before dusk, he gave a polite knock on the door.

"Come on in." We walked him to the backyard.

"What a gorgeous place you have here. Who built your treehouse?" he inquired.

We responded simultaneously, "We built it with our daddies."

"Your dads are very talented men, and they are blessed to have two helpful daughters like you." After we took him on a tour of the backyard and the treehouse, he offered some advice. "My only suggestion for you is to be careful each time you enter your treehouse. I don't see any critters. However, if you come across any, call me. I have a team who can safely relocate them to a new home away from your property."

"Mr. O'Conner, can I ask you a curious question?"

"Of course, Faith, what's on your mind?"

I continued, "You mentioned last night that you help trees. Do you believe that trees have feelings?"

Mr. O'Conner hesitated a moment before he answered, "That's not a silly question at all. Can you explain why you're asking, Faith?"

"I ask because the night I broke my arm, I had a dream while I was in surgery. Do you see where the branches were removed?" I pointed to the scars on the tree. "Those scars look like a face to me."

Mr. O'Conner explained, "Those are actually called cicatrix, or calluses."

I confided in him, "Well, in my dream, Old Solomon's cicatrix face came to life. He didn't seem very happy and said some things to me that I haven't stopped thinking about ever since. I know it was just a dream, but I can't help but wonder if it meant something more. Could it be possible that we caused him pain?"

Mr. O'Conner knew exactly what I was talking about. He, too, has a connection to nature that makes him more sensitive to protecting it. He answered, "Faith, your dream is very interesting to me. What specifically did he say to you?"

"I'm embarrassed to admit that Old Solomon scolded me for my behavior," I answered, surprised that he wanted to know more. "I was being disobedient when I broke my arm."

Mr. O'Conner shook his head as if he was sure that he knew why I dreamed about Old Solomon's appearance in my dream.

Before he could speak, I felt the need to explain myself, saying, "Dezzie and I planned this treehouse for several years. We never thought about how Old Solomon felt about it. Now, I'm wondering if we should have researched more about trees and less about the treehouse because Old Solomon was seriously not happy about my behavior. I'm afraid I have stressed him out."

Dezzie was taken aback and asked, "Faith, why haven't you shared this with me?"

I admitted, "Dezzie, I'm sorry I didn't tell you. I didn't know what to think about it myself."

Mr. O'Conner appreciated our concern for Old Solomon and gave us his best explanation, concluding, "Faith, trees are plants, and plants don't have brains or a nervous system; therefore, they don't have feelings. However, there are theories that prove stress has an effect on trees. Trees are good to us. After all, they provide us with shade, food, and, most importantly, oxygen. I will add that humans and plants have similar needs– sun, air, and water. We have a lot in common. As for Old Solomon here, I personally think he is honored to have the name of the most wise Old Testament king in the Bible. He appears to be the most noble tree in your backyard and, more than that, honored to hold your treehouse. Your dream was just that, Faith, just a dream."

"Thanks so much, Mr. O'Conner. I hope you're right," I said, relieved that I wasn't on Old Solomon's bad side.

Mr. O'Conner posed a question to us, changing the subject and saying, "I read the email from Mrs. Diamond. I noticed your name is Daddy's Angels. I find that intriguing. I used to watch Charlie's Angels, so I appreciate the clever wordplay, girls. I also noticed that you've named your treehouse the Bright Light Treehouse. Would you mind sharing the story behind that name?"

Dezzie responded, "Certainly, sir. We combined our last names for it. Faith's last name is Joule, which represents energy in light, while my last name is Diamond, shining the light. Together, we form a bright light, and this is our house. It's simple, really."

"I like it," Mr. O'Conner nodded in approval. "I believe you'll discover this name will carry even more significance in the future. The scientist in me is tempted to explain photosynthesis to you both. It's a big word, but I think you'll find it interesting to learn how crucial it is for Old Solomon here."

Dezzie responded, "Mr. O'Conner, science is my favorite subject, and I'm currently studying photosynthesis. You can help tutor me so I'll make a good grade on my test."

Mr. O'Conner, honored to have our full attention, began to explain, "The sun's light provides Old Solomon here the energy he needs to survive. That energy undergoes a transformation into chemical energy, which is stored and later used for his growth. Light is crucial for the development of his leaves and branches."

We nodded, indicating our interest even though we didn't grasp all the details. Eager for more information, we chimed in, "Mr. O'Conner, please continue."

"If Old Solomon here doesn't receive adequate light, he will struggle to produce leaves and branches, and he'll weaken over time. Light is the source of his vitality. Your decision to name the treehouse the Bright Light Treehouse may indeed be a significant help to him. Not only does he take pride in hosting you, but in a way, you're also supporting his well-being."

"Mr. O'Conner, that's wonderful to hear. I feel sure I'll make a better grade on my test now that you have explained photosynthesis to us. It is a big word with a simple meaning: light gives life. Got it."

Dezzie shook Mr. O'Conner's hand and expressed, "Mr. O'Conner, you've been a great help to us two days straight. If it weren't for Daddy's Angels, we might never have met you. Faith has a theory that everyone we encounter has a purpose. I genuinely believe we met you for this very reason. Your reassurance about Old Solomon's approval of our Bright Light Treehouse has truly brightened my day. If there is anything we can do for you, please don't hesitate to let us know."

Mr. O'Conner smiled, visibly touched by our words. As he contemplated how we might return the favor, he replied, "Let me consider your offer. It's gardening time at our house, and I'm sure we can come up with something worthwhile for you to assist me with. I must be on my way. Mrs. O'Conner is expecting me home for supper."

Walking over to the gate to wave goodbye, Dezzie said, "Today has been a good day as Daddy's Angels, hasn't it? We learned a lot, that's for sure. First, we learned about sliding into home plate and reproduction, then we fed newborn puppies for the first time, and now," she gave me a disapproving look for not telling her about my dream, "Old Solomon talks to you in your dreams?"

"Dezzie, I didn't say anything to you about Old Solomon because I was afraid that you might question my dream. I lacked proof, and I didn't want to argue with you only for you to prove me wrong. I'm so sorry for not not sharing this with you earlier." Changing the subject, I offered a favor, "If it will make you feel better, I'll call Mom to come over, and we can ask our moms how babies are made. They definitely have some explaining to do. I think they owe us a puppy for not telling us sooner. Surely, they can't deny us both a puppy."

Dezzie chuckled and said, "You know, Faith, getting a puppy would definitely make me feel better. How about we talk to our moms separately and then compare notes tomorrow? I don't know if we can believe Georgia."

"Secret handshake and a hug for a day to remember?" I said

"Absolutely." Dezzie extended her right arm and then her left, remembering my cast.

"The secret handshake doesn't feel right with the left hand. We'll have to practice tomorrow so we can get better at it."

Looking back at Old Solomon, pointing with my left hand and giving him an overemphasized wink, I said, "I'll see you in my dreams."

Dezzie said, "Faith Joule, you're a nut. Let's go home."

Walking home, I had an epiphany. If miracles cannot be explained, then my dream was certainly a miracle. I was convinced, without a doubt, that Old Solomon talked to me. Now that Mr. O'Conner has confirmed that it wasn't possible for a tree to talk. That cemented my belief in Old Solomon's conversation all the more. I was hoping he would meet me in my dreams again.

I returned home and headed to bed early, my mind swirling with the day's revelations. Mom walked in. "Hey, Angel. I haven't seen you all day. Can I get a hug before you go to sleep?"

"Mom, we need to talk," I said as I set my journal and pen aside.

"Sure honey, what about? You know you can talk to me about anything."

I sat straight up and said, "Tell me again how babies are made."

"Well, I guess you are getting old enough to know all of the details, and you live in a house full of teenagers, so they'll be telling you sooner or later. I would rather you hear it from me."

Mom shared with me precisely what Georgia had told us about reproduction, emphasizing that it was a sacred act of marriage. I asked her, "What does it feel like to have a baby in your stomach?"

She answered, "It's like preparing for Christmas morning. There's a gift growing inside of you, but you can't unwrap it until it's time." She delved deeper into the details of pregnancy, the doctor's office visits, nausea, discomfort, and the pain of childbirth.

"God must have been really angry at Eve. No wonder they call it 'The Fall of Man.'" I lamented.

"Well, there's no need to mourn," she responded. "The good news is, it's not all that bad. Every aspect of God's creation is beautiful, even reproduction. You're correct that we're still living out Eve's punishment for giving Adam the forbidden fruit, enduring the hardships of childbirth. But, Faith, thousands of babies are born all over the world each day. Once you become a mother, you'll forget the hard parts of pregnancy when you hold your beautiful miracle baby in your arms."

"I don't know how you did that four times. If I've never told you, thank you for having me." We hugged.

"You're our treasure, Faith. Truly, you are an immense blessing to your daddy and me. We love you very much. I'm glad you asked me about reproduction. I've been wanting to tell you but didn't know when the right time would be. Now that you know, it's important that you also learn the sanctity of marriage and childbearing. The blessing of family is one of the greatest gifts. Faith, it's never too early to start praying for your future husband and your children. In time, God's time, you will know who and when to marry and start a family. But for now, you can learn how to be a mighty woman for God. Then you'll be prepared for marriage and motherhood."

She continued, "In fact, the church is hosting a class for middle and high schoolers starting Wednesday nights. It's called Purity of Heart, Mind, and Body. Our new Children's minister, Grace, is going to teach the girls. I've signed you up. It covers God's plan for purity of the body as a whole. I've talked with Moriah, and she is going to allow Dezzie to attend the class with you."

"Mom, you don't have to worry about my purity. I'm not having children any time soon. I'll reconsider pregnancy if I get married. I have another question, though. You often say, 'Babies are miracles.' How can you call the process a miracle if it is determined by humans?"

"Good question, I'm glad you asked," she replied. "From the moment the sperm and the egg are released, their delicate journey can face obstacles anywhere along the way. The fact that these two elements can meet, fertilize, and thrive is indeed a miracle. Then, the healthy growth within the womb for nine months is another miracle. During that time, the baby floats in a fluid that nourishes them until they are born and takes their first breath."

Remembering the miracle of birth, Mom continued, "Yes, love, God's mighty outstretched hand is on each conception, pregnancy, and birth. We are all 'knitted in our mother's womb' as the Psalms tell us. Do you know anyone who can make a human body with all the intricate details? I certainly don't. Only God can do that."

"Speaking of babies, Dezzie and I have been feeding the neighbor's puppies because the mama dog is lost. They are so cute," I said, changing the subject. "I sure would like to have a puppy. Mrs. Boutwell is saving three of them. One for Dezzie, one for Georgia, and one for me."

"Oh Faith, I swore I would never raise another puppy," Mom exhaled as the words tumbled out. She sounded defeated just thinking about it.

"He wouldn't be yours, Mom. He would be mine, all mine. I'm totally responsible enough for a puppy," I declared.

She tried her best to talk me out of it, saying, "An active puppy requires a lot of attention. He'll keep you up at night, and you know how grumpy you are when you haven't had enough sleep."

"I wouldn't be grumpy if I had a puppy. That would make me happy."

"No matter how tired from the night before, you would have to get up early with the dog every day to feed and walk him before any other school or activities, even on the weekends. It's never-ending. They don't take a day off, and they have a ton of energy."

"I'm an early bird, Mom. You know that would not be a problem at all."

She continued, "If you leave him without boundaries, he will be messy, chew your favorite shoes, eat your furniture, and no telling what else, but he will be yours, and you will love him anyway."

"Are you saying I can get one?" I asked.

"No, I didn't say that. I need to ask your dad first. But, Faith, if he says yes, I'm serious, this puppy will be your full responsibility."

"Thanks, Mom. Before you leave and go to bed, is there anything else you haven't told me?"

She smiled, "We would be up all night if I told you everything. You look tired. Get some rest. I think that's enough news for today."

I went to sleep dreaming of puppies licking my face.

The following morning was a Sunday. Dezzie and I usually didn't talk until after lunch on Sundays, but I was dying to know how her conversation went with her mom. I woke up early, before the sun came up, darted across the street, and tapped on her window. Dezzie lifted her window and rubbed her eyes. "Faith, what are you doing over here so early?"

"We need to compare notes. Mom told me everything about how babies are made, one hundred percent. From the beginning to the end, I heard it all."

"Meet me around back. We'll talk in the treehouse so we don't wake anyone," Dezzie said.

I met Dezzie at the side gate where she let me in. She stretched. "Faith, this couldn't wait until this afternoon?"

"Dezzie, this is important. I want to know what your mom said."

In the treehouse, I looked at Old Solomon's scarred face and believed that he was listening to our conversation. Oh, the secrets he will know from our Bright Light Treehouse meetings.

"You go first." Dezzie yawned, pulled her blanket up and around her shoulders, and said, "I'm too tired to talk."

"Well, my mom told me everything that Georgia told us and more. She showed me a cool 3D video on how the egg and sperm are fertilized and another one about the baby growing in the mom's tummy. Then, she told me about how pregnancy changes a woman's body as the baby grows and develops. Did you know we start out as a tiny human cell? That was almost too much for my pea brain to understand. She told me about morning sickness, gaining weight, her back hurting, swollen feet, and the awful pain of childbirth. Then, she told me about taking me home to feed and change a lot of nasty diapers. I never thought about the sleepless nights spent caring for a newborn. I'm definitely not in a hurry to have a baby, but I am one hundred percent ready for a puppy."

Dezzie agreed, saying, "Yeah, I mean, exactly. My mom said that she couldn't have children for a long time even though she and my dad weren't," she paused and held up her quotation fingers and said, 'preventing it,' whatever that means. She said that when she finally had Bianca, she thought Bianca was going to be an only child. She was an only child until I was born six years later. Mom said that since God gave her two of the best girls in the world, she was grateful. Isn't that sweet? She also said that I was a miracle baby. She's never told me that before. I loved hearing her say that about me. You know Faith, I'm really glad we asked our moms about this. They're so busy working to care for us in the present, they rarely talk about the past. My mom smiled the whole time she talked about being pregnant. I think having babies made her very happy."

"As happy as it would make us to have a puppy?" I asked.

"I asked her about getting a puppy. She wasn't very excited about it at first, but the more we talked, the more positive she was. She realized that raising a puppy would offer an excellent opportunity to practice responsibility. She's going to ask Dad. How about your mom?"

"Same, she has to have Dad's permission. Wouldn't it be fun if our dogs were official Daddy's Angels, assisting us in all of our missions? We'll train them to be good detectives."

"Left hand high five and secret handshake!"

CHAPTER 9

MEETING GRACE

Dezzie and I attended different churches. We didn't ever visit each other's church on Sunday mornings, but when either church hosted a special event, we would sometimes attend as a guest. Having a friend to share a potentially uncomfortable experience can make it much more bearable.

On the drive to church that Wednesday night, we attempted to change Mom's mind. "Do we really have to go? We would love to have time to discuss some things about purity privately with you. We still have questions. You can answer all our questions. I mean, why would we need to go to a class when you can tell us? Honestly, Mom, we're twelve. We're pretty confident that we're not going to have babies any time soon, I promise. Look at us, Mom. We consider ourselves to be very responsible for twelve-year-olds, even managing a charitable volunteer service."

"First of all, I'm flattered that you want to spend more time with me. We'll have a girl's day out soon. However, tonight, you two are going to purity class. These classes help you understand the 'why' we should strive to stay pure as Christians. It's like crossing the street, girls. Remember when we used to tell you to 'stop, look, and listen before crossing'? It wasn't just for nothing. Right? We were teaching you safety, so that you didn't get run smack over by a car. This purity class will guide you in making thoughtful decisions. Remember, our thoughts have a significant impact on our actions."

Our awkward silence caused Mom to elaborate on her point.

Mom empathized with our concerns, saying, "Girls, you're definitely on the right path, and I'm incredibly proud of you. This class will only increase your understanding of the significance of your pure thoughts, words, and actions. It's not just about starting a family; it's a fundamental part of your Christian faith. This class will take you on a deeper dive into understanding how seriously God regards holiness."

Confused, I asked, "Why would anyone choose anything other than purity?"

Mom agreed, "I share the same concern, Faith. A weak mind that lacks clarity is easily manipulated by the enemy. Just as we exercise our body for physical strength, we must also nurture our spiritual mind for mental resilience. If Satan gains control of a weak mind, he can lead that person down a destructive path. However, what's even more crucial is the victory we achieve when he cannot steal our hearts and minds. We belong to God, so we dedicate our minds and bodies entirely to Him, from head to toe."

She continued, "When I was your age, I attended purity class. It's improved a lot since then. I recently attended the parent orientation meeting here at the church, where they answered our questions about the content of this class. This is a redesigned and enhanced purity class. Unlike the previous one, which primarily focused on physical self-protection, this class emphasizes serving Jesus. True purity deals with more than just our physical bodies; it extends to the heart and mind, prioritizing our relationship with Him above all others. Then, we go forth in our purity without fear and shame, but in service to Jesus."

She giggled, "I guess I could help teach the class. You girls have caused me to stretch my spiritual muscles today. As always, you'll be great students. On another note, I want you to welcome Grace, our new children's minister. She holds two college degrees as well as solid theological and child developmental experience. Not only is she highly recommended for her position by her colleagues and professors, but her previous employer said she's a natural with girls your age. I look forward to getting to know her soon also."

When Mom dropped us off, there was a beautiful girl at the entrance waving and smiling. She introduced herself, "Hi, I'm Grace." She welcomed us and immediately gave us a job. She must have sensed our willingness to be helpful. She informed us, saying, "We're expecting a large crowd, so I'm glad you got here a little early to help me. Will you please be sure everyone signs in, gets a name tag, a handout, and a pen?"

Once everyone was settled, we took two of the seats on the front row that Grace saved for us. Grace led our group with confidence. Her natural beauty shone through her modest casual attire. Her loose-fitting jeans paired with running shoes and an oversized t-shirt with our church's logo were completely appropriate for our youth meeting on purity. She didn't address us like a teacher. Instead, she spoke to us as if she had already been our longtime friend. In fact, I could envision myself looking a lot like her when I get to be her age. Her hair was a lighter shade of blond, with a sassy side braid cascading down her back. Her slender yet strong physique, although hidden underneath her clothes, hinted at a passion for running.

She expressed her excitement at being a new member of our church and how much she looked forward to getting to know each of us individually. She handed out cards with her name and phone number on it, telling us that she would be calling us to schedule lunch over the summer.

Her introduction to the purity class involved a science experiment aimed at illustrating how Jesus washes our sins away. On stage was a table with a white table cloth, and some supplies that looked like a chemistry lab. Grace introduced the evening's topic, saying, "Tonight, we are going to start our purity class with a visual to demonstrate Jesus's power to take away our sins."

Dezzie's hand shot up swiftly when Grace requested a volunteer. Once she was on stage, another ministry intern brought out two jars of clear liquid. One flask was labeled "sin," and the other was labeled "you." When Dezzie poured the clear liquid of the "sin" jar into the clear liquid of the "you" jar, the clear liquid turned red. In turn, she poured the red "you" liquid into the "sin" jar; all of the liquid in those two jars remained a vivid shade of red. Gasps filled the room because there was no red dye anywhere. We all wondered how the liquid turned red without an added ingredient. All eyes were on the stage.

Grace paused the experiment, explaining, "No matter how hard you try to get sin out of your life, you cannot accomplish sinlessness on your own."

Then, she brought out an old-fashioned straw dispenser with a chrome-plated top. A foam cutout of a cross was taped to the rod that held the base. She handed that to Dezzie, instructing her to insert it inside the "you" jar. The red liquid became clear once again. Next, she had Dezzie pour the red "sin" liquid into the clear "you" jar, and all of the liquid became clear.

Grace noticed the amazement on all of our faces, and she proceeded to clarify the demonstration, saying, "This is a representation of the transformative power of Jesus in our lives. Even when we try to combat sin on our own, we stumble and fall short. However, when we invite Jesus into our lives, we are cleansed and purified, made clean and forgiven. With Jesus, sin loses its grip on us. Even in the eyes of God, we are seen as pure and holy. His presence within us prevents sin from staining us any longer. The Bible says we are washed white as snow through the shedding of Jesus's blood, which purifies us."

Grace asked, "Anyone else want to try it?"

Several hands shot up. The children's leaders repeated the experiment two more times to drive home the impact. As a visual learner, this demonstration left a lasting impression on me and made the concept of sanctification much clearer. For years, I sat in Sunday School and church, wondering if it could truly apply for someone like me. However, after seeing this experiment, I was certain it was a reality for anyone who accepted Jesus.

Grace introduced one of the other children's ministers, Chad. He'd been working as the sole children's minister at the church for many years. Our church has increased in attendance, almost twice the members. It had grown so quickly over the last few years, he needed some assistance, so they hired Grace. Chad announced that the girls were going to stay in the auditorium with Grace while the boys were going to follow him into the gym.

As soon as all the boys left the room, Dezzie raised her hand before Grace had an opportunity to start the class. "Yes, do you have a question?"

Dezzie declared, "That experiment you used seems like a magic trick. My mom says I'm a gifted child, smarter than most. I know that there is an order in science. After all, even God used order to create the universe, not magic. So, if it's not too much trouble, could you please give me the chemical composition of the liquids you used in those reactions? I don't mean to come across as skeptical, but I believe we can't rely solely on reason to draw conclusions about purity. I would like some empirical evidence to support the idea that I'm pure even though I've accepted Jesus. I would like to see the research."

Grace used this opportunity to emphasize her lesson on purity, remarking, "Dezzie, I genuinely value your inquisitive nature. Please do follow your research wherever it leads you. However, there are no surgical heart biopsies for our spirits, so tangible proof in the traditional sense is not available. You'll need to rely on faith to believe that purity exists, much like it takes faith to believe in Jesus and his holy Word, the Bible."

Grace continued her teaching, looking at everyone and explaining, "The demonstration served as a visual representation of our hearts when we accept Christ. Let me clarify using another analogy. Consider the element of gold." She took off her ring and held it up for all to see. "The reason gold holds such value is because it is pure gold, with no other elements mixed in. It's one hundred percent gold, completely whole."

"Similarly, in the Christian life, a pure heart is wholly dedicated to Jesus, one hundred percent. To achieve purity of heart, we make the daily choice to focus on Him. How can we do that? Well, one way is through prayer. Another way is reading the Bible daily. We can also maintain fellowship with other believers, such as attending church and participating in Bible studies. Can anyone else think of a way to stay pure?"

Dezzie held up her hand again. This has certainly tickled her science bone, piquing her curiosity, commenting, "My last name is Diamond. I've done research and science experiments with diamonds. My mom has even taken me on a field trip to a jewelry store. Did you know that the rarest of all the diamonds is a flawless one? It's purely carbon, the hardest naturally occurring substance known."

I looked at Dezzie and whispered, "That was off-subject. If we keep interrupting her, she's going to start ignoring us. I don't think you answered her question correctly."

I then looked at Grace and gave an apologetic smile. Grace responded with warmth as if it was just the two of them in the room and patiently responded, saying, "Dezzie, in God's eyes, you are a flawless diamond."

Dezzie was deeply moved. Her eyes filled up with tears.

That night, I realized that Grace was a remarkably wise children's minister, and I eagerly anticipated our upcoming lunch together.

We ended the night with another visual. Grace brought out two large jars of honey with some snacks. She explained honey is a worldwide treat. It's mentioned in the Bible sixty-one times. Not only is honey delicious, but it contains antioxidants, vitamins, and minerals that heal our bodies.

"Pure honey, much like pure people, is not easy to distinguish by appearance alone. In fact, only God created us and knows if an individual is pure. So, if a person doesn't believe in God or care about godly principles, purity doesn't matter. Purity is a distinguishing trait of a Christian. It's a trait worth working towards, much like worker bees must put forth the work to make pure honey.

"Next time you're in the grocery store with your parents, go look at the honey on the shelf. Try to determine by the label if you can see the difference. Some honey in the store has become adulterated or mixed with synthetic products, sweeteners, and contaminants to add to its composition, making it no longer pure and not as healthy.

"I want to know if you can determine which honey is the purely natural honey and which is the synthetic variety. The jars are covered with paper and numbered with a "one" or a "two." I want you to write down the number of the jar you choose, then comment whether it is natural or synthetic, pure or not pure."

Grace had pretzels out for us to dip in the honey that we chose to taste. You could hear everyone talking about the delicious honey once they compared the two choices. "This is definitely the pure one," or "I can't really taste the difference." I heard one person saying out loud, "In my own opinion, the pure honey was much sweeter."

Grace announced, "Once everyone has finished taste testing, I'll show you how you can know if the honey is pure or not."

She brought out a bowl of water. She held up a jar of honey labeled with number one, saying, "Do you think this honey is pure?"

Many "No" answers were called out, with some "yes" votes.

She added a spoonful of honey to the water. "The honey dissolved quickly in the water," she explained. "This honey is not pure. It dissolves quickly because it has added ingredients like sugar, which dissolves quickly in water."

She held up the jar of honey labeled number two. Again, she added a spoonful of honey to a new bowl of water, which fell to the bottom of the bowl. She said, "This honey doesn't dissolve in the water because it is pure."

Grace elaborated, "My family owns a honeybee farm. These are my daddy's small jars of honey for you all to take home. I pray it reminds you to stay pure and sweet as pure honey."

After her honey experiment, she closed in prayer. Many of us stayed and visited while we snacked on more pure honey. It was delicious.

"Bye, Grace, my mom is here to get us," I told her. I gave her a side hug and told her how glad we are that she's teaching our class, saying, "Welcome to our church. I'm very glad you're here."

Once we got in the car, we showed Mom our free honey and told her all about the night. "Well, girls, I assumed you would be the first two to run out of the church. I have been here waiting for over fifteen minutes. Are you still convinced that you don't need a purity class?" Mom sarcastically asked us on our drive home.

"I can't wait to get back next week. I really like Grace," I responded.

"Me too. Can you believe what she said to me? I'm a flawless diamond," Dezzie said.

She glowed as she absorbed Grace's charge over her. I never realized how a simple yet profound, sincere compliment can impact someone, especially from someone who is older and wiser. I made a mental note to myself, saying, "When you get older, be sure to compliment young girls who are in your care so they too can feel loved."

CHAPTER 10

OLD SOLOMON'S WORDS OF WISDOM

I went to bed that night thinking about the purity class. I prayed, "Dear Jesus, help me to be pure in heart, mind, and body." Deep into the night, in my deepest sleep, I dreamed I was talking to Old Solomon again. I found myself perched in the treehouse, bathed in the light of the moon. The shadows danced and waved with the rhythm of the wind. Alone in this tranquil space, my gaze was fixed on Old Solomon's gnarled trunk. Though I kept my voice hushed, I spoke aloud, silently hoping that Old Solomon could hear my words.

"Old Solomon, I attended a purity class tonight. I'm learning about my thoughts and my actions. I feel like we added to your splendor, and now we have made you impure. We learned that additives in natural honey make it less healthy. Old Solomon, I would have never added the treehouse to your canopy if I knew that it would hurt you. I really hope that we haven't caused you harm."

Without a response from Old Solomon, the silence was more than uncomfortable, so I kept talking, saying, "Mom always tells us to treat everyone as we would like to be treated, and maybe we didn't consider your feelings enough. Honestly, I never thought that you would have an opinion about hosting the treehouse until the night of my surgery when you spoke to me in my dream. You seemed upset with me for breaking my arm. But as I reflected on it more, I realized that your frustration wasn't only about me neglecting my family and Dezzie but also about me overlooking your feelings. Your words sounded like something my parents would say as if you were warning me about my lack of appreciation for others and possibly for yourself."

Old Solomon was unresponsive, but I was determined, so I kept talking, asking, "Would it be helpful to know that we chose you because of your strength and beauty? In my children's Bible, King Solomon is tall, dark, handsome, and powerful, just like you are. You are the most sturdy tree in the yard. I'm really sorry for not asking you first, but honestly, it never crossed my mind."

Old Solomon's silence was unbearable, so I kept talking, saying, "I met a neighbor, Mr. O'Conner, who is a specialist in trees. I asked him to examine you for predators. He says you're in tip top shape, able to hold a treehouse. He's also aware of our conversation in my dream. I told him that you seemed irritated by my actions and that you scorned me for ignoring my sister's and my friend's advice. Old Solomon, I always assumed trees were big plants without feelings until you spoke to me. According to Mr. O'Conner's research, you don't have a brain, and therefore, you don't have feelings. However, I know that you spoke to me with very strong feelings on the night that I broke my arm. You spoke as if you valued me enough to tell me the harsh truth."

I glanced away, pondering whether Old Solomon had even heard my words. Then, I turned my gaze back toward him, wanting to repeat just how sorry I was for my selfishness. "Hindsight, as they say, is twenty-twenty. If only we could turn back time, we would have asked your permission to place our treehouse in your majestic branches from the start."

As I continued to speak, a peculiar thing happened. The imperfections and blemishes on Old Solomon's trunk began to shift and move. He let out what seemed like a yawn, and his expression, while no longer angry, remained far from jovial. Instead, it seemed he found my presence and words somewhat amusing as if my heartfelt conversation with him had struck a chord.

Old Solomon spoke with gracious wisdom. "Faith, I've been around for over nine hundred years, and if there's one thing an old tree enjoys, it's witnessing young, innocent children play and revel in nature's beauty. You and Dezzie remind me of my own youth when I sprouted from a tiny acorn and began growing into a young tree. In those early years, I imagined myself achieving great feats in service to my fellow creatures. I imagined myself providing them with shelter and sustenance, caring for insects and mammals alike. Yet, sadly, I've seen many of my companions taken away to destinations unknown. Letting go is an inevitable part of life, and I had to learn to let them go while I remained rooted here. I was chosen to be admired, all while using what I had been given to be useful for other purposes," he replied with wisdom that surprised me.

I closed my eyes tight, keeping them closed for a few seconds as I rolled my eyeballs around to clean off the crusties in my eyes that may cause irregular shadows or imaginary visions. "Old Solomon, I'm a little freaked out here. Are you real, or are you in my dream?" I asked him.

He chuckled, "I am as real as this treehouse in my branches, and I'm also in your dream."

"Trees don't talk, at least not in real life," I argued.

"Faith, do you believe in God and the Bible?" Old Solomon asked.

Yes, sir, I do. I've accepted Jesus into my heart, and I'll be baptized soon. I've gone to Sunday school and church my whole life," I answered with confidence.

"So you're familiar with the Garden of Eden, created by God for Adam and all of mankind. The Garden's Tree of Life is my great-great-great-great-great-grandfather. I'm in his family tree, no pun intended. And in our family line, some of us have been assigned to help God's children," Old Solomon said with seriousness in his voice.

"Old Solomon, I heard the Garden of Eden was destroyed in the great flood during Noah's time. Your ancestors would have been destroyed too," I protested.

"Yes, that's how we were dispersed from there to here, by the great flood. The flood, although tragic, allowed for vegetation to spread over the earth. All suffering, in due time, allows for growth. Faith, there is a crossroads in every child's life when they discover the evil in the world. Don't forget these words that I'm sharing with you. God has a plan and purpose for your life to serve Him and others."

"If you are real, then what were Dezzie and I talking about last Sunday morning when we came to the treehouse?" I asked, testing him.

"You were talking about a conversation that you had with your moms about babies and puppies," he answered.

"This is so weird. Nobody is going to believe that I'm talking to a tree, much less a nine hundred-year-old-tree. Are you really that old? I asked.

"I'm not old, Faith, I'm ancient." He continued, "I've experienced harsh winter seasons, blazing summers, and uncontrollably painful falls. I have observed my family transition each spring, shedding our leaves only to start anew each year. With the warmth of summer, our lower branches would receive less sunlight, and we would experience a different kind of loss. Life's lessons hit me like a lightning strike in the storms of existence. However, the later years of my life have been the most rewarding. When I look back over the healing moments of my long existence, I can see the fruits of my resilience through tribulations. The joy of entertaining people like your family, becoming a neighborhood icon, has taught me to appreciate my place in this world. I've learned to adapt to the circumstances I find myself in." Old Solomon's words were a testament to his enduring wisdom and the lessons learned over centuries of existence. His insights were like a precious gift. I started believing him instead of denying his existence.

"Faith, I am truly honored that you and Dezzie chose me to host your treehouse. It's the most substantial 'nest' I've ever had the privilege to hold. Fortunately, I've grown stronger over the years, and surviving and conquering the challenges of my past has contributed to the tree I've become today. I've become more flexible and adaptable, a quality I didn't always possess. I learned that harboring grudges only led to the growth of bitter roots that weakened my trunk and stunted my progress. However, nourishing myself with living water and basking in the sun's warmth helped me to replace those bitter roots with healthier ones," Old Solomon explained.

"I've been a keen observer my entire existence, witnessing and experiencing the natural changes that unfold around me. As

I watch you and Dezzie play, taking risks that many young girls might never consider, I see immense potential in you both. However, young lady, you need to harness that boundless energy and direct it toward doing good rather than causing harm to yourself and others," Solomon advised

"Old Solomon, I don't want to disappoint you. I'm trying. I really am. I've even given Dezzie permission to tell me, 'Let's go home' when I get out of line or spin off course."

Solomon continued, "Observe Dezzie as she thoughtfully contemplates her next move. She, much like a tree, takes her time. If you continue to rush through life without considering the potential consequences, you might miss out on some of the most significant moments. You are constantly in motion, rushing from one moment to the next, and in doing so, you might not fully experience the present. Your zest for life can be a great asset, but it's crucial to learn how to pause and reflect before you act."

"My ears are open, Old Solomon. Please continue," I encouraged, eager to absorb more of his wisdom.

"Faith, if you are willing to heed my guidance, you will grow in wisdom and discover your purpose. Your innate generosity will lead you to become a compassionate woman, sharing the beautiful parts of you everywhere you go. I envision you, much like a tree, providing shelter for those less fortunate. You'll encounter loss, just as I have, but you will heal and emerge even stronger in the aftermath of adversity. You, Faith, will offer refuge for those in search of it. You'll provide solace, sustenance, and a brighter future. You'll be a source of beauty not just for others to admire but to learn from. All this will unfold if you allow yourself to slow down, observe, and learn from the changes that surround you," Old Solomon conveyed with profound, insightful foresight.

I asked him, "Old Solomon, can you please tell me more about the losses I might experience?"

Solomon responded. "I can't predict the specific losses you might face, but I can certainly guide you on how to rise above them. As long as we keep our hearts lifted in worship to Him, He will help us deal with whatever comes our way."

Intrigued, I asked, "Old Solomon, why would a tree die if it has the ability to heal itself?"

Old Solomon replied, "A tree shortens its own life when it fails to allocate sufficient internal resources or seek assistance from other parts, like leaves and roots, to heal its wounds. Without help, the injury can become infected, festering until the tree perishes from the inside out. As for you, you may encounter injuries that could harm the most crucial parts within you. Your childlike belief in all that is good and right in the world might be wounded, perhaps by someone you love. This could potentially lead to lifelong harm or even emotional devastation unless you make a conscious effort to heal promptly," Solomon's words resonated in my mind.

"You're scaring me now, Old Solomon. I don't understand why someone who loves me would hurt me," I admitted.

He continued, "You see, Faith, while I lack many of the organs that humans possess, I have a unique rhythm within me, much like your heartbeat. I send signals and circulate chemicals to aid in healing my branches and fostering new growth. The tree you see today has had to exert tremendous effort to reach this point of incredible strength and unwavering resilience. I've faced countless challenges and nearly perished many times, but I persevered, putting in the hard work to mend both the broken and wounded parts, both within and without. Recovery is a process that takes time, and it's important for you to be patient with yourself as you navigate your own journey."

"Are you talking about my broken arm or something worse?" I asked. Old Solomon's words left me with a sense of unease and curiosity. I contemplated what kind of pain he was referring to.

I didn't like pain. I sat there, fear gripping me as I contemplated my own vulnerabilities and the possibility of experiencing hurt. I don't want to think about how to heal myself from the inside out. I liked the thought of helping others, but I never thought that I would need help.

"Can't I avoid the pain and the potential harm that might threaten me?" I asked.

He met my question with a serious expression, his tree-like demeanor unchanging. "No, Faith, you can't avoid it. There is no true strength without enduring pain. Take your broken arm, for example. You experienced pain, and now, your arm is healing. It will mend over time, and you'll use that arm again.

"Many have tried to sidestep suffering, but it's one of the greatest mysteries of creation. Just as trees must seek help when injured, you humans have your own resources - counselors, pastors, doctors, friends, and family. You have numerous opportunities for healing, but if you don't utilize them, you'll continue to suffer. Prolonged suffering can break you down from the inside out, and I've witnessed the consequences of bitter roots. They're far from pleasant. Those who isolate themselves in pain can turn to poisons that only prolong and compound their issues, making healing harder. Your purpose, Faith, is to navigate through the hard times. You'll heal and grow, and then, you'll help others to heal and grow. Don't lose hope. The trees that bear the most fruit are the ones that never lose hope," Solomon advised with wisdom that both challenged and comforted me.

CHAPTER 11

FAITH'S CHILDHOOD TRAUMA

Old Solomon's image seemed to blur, and my senses were jolted awake. Amidst the haze, I heard three words echoing as if they were resounding through a distant tunnel, "Never lose hope."

I heard someone in the bathroom, then the toilet flushed. It was Hunt, Aaron's friend and my emergency Uber ambulance driver, who swept me up on the day I broke my arm. He was walking down the hallway when I opened my bedroom door. I overheard the boys making plans to sit outside with some of the girls in the neighborhood, including Dezzie's sister, Bianca. It wasn't unusual for the teenagers to stay up late, but it seemed later than usual.

"Hey Aaron, is it alright if I just stay the night?" Hunt said to Aaron as he walked outside.

I thought about hiding behind the curtain and watching, ever curious about what teenagers do that late at night. But Aaron would be mad at me if he caught me spying on them, so I went back to my room. I could see the patio light reflecting off of my dresser mirror, and I could hear music and their muffled voices. The cuckoo clock in the den rang out at midnight with twelve calls of the "cuckoo." I closed the door, took a sip of water from the glass at my bedside, and crawled underneath the covers. Later, I heard cars drive off. Then, the quiet of the night began again.

I must have dozed off. I was in and out of sleep, warmer than usual. I wanted to throw off the blanket that was so heavy, but then I realized it wasn't a blanket. My body went rigid, and my heart raced within my chest. There was someone else nearby. Before I dared to open my eyes, I took a deep breath, inhaling an unforgettable skunk-like scent. He was sweaty, breathing heavily, and touching me. I went in and out of sleep, slowly realizing that this wasn't a dream. All of a sudden, I was wide awake. I silently panicked. I pretended I was still asleep. I started to tremble, and I wanted to cry. I could hear my heart banging in my chest.

I froze, telling myself, "Don't move. Just be still." I barely opened my eyes, seeing that there was very little light in my room, but the glow of the night light cast a silhouette on Hunt's profile. I closed my eyes. I didn't want to see anything else.

I remember when he drove me to the hospital on the day that I experienced the worst pain of my life. He was so nice. He even said I was like a little sister to him when he signed my cast. How could he hurt me like this? He knew that I was incapable of protecting myself. Then I prayed, "Lord, please make him stop."

I remembered Old Solomon's words in my dream, "You will experience loss."

I was so confused. *Why was this happening to me? Why was he doing this to me?*

I knew this was bad. I knew this was very wrong.

"Lord, please help me," I prayed.

I can't fully explain what happened next. I've heard that our brains are like computers. When they crash, there's a hardware failure or power outage. That night, my brain crashed, much like a computer. I lost access to my ability to fight back. Any promise that I made to Dezzie to face danger or Bible verse that I memorized about fighting battles was gone. That Daddy's Angel and warrior of God, left the scene of the crime. That girl who wanted to save the world could not even save herself. That girl that was going to face danger when everyone else fled, she fled too. I blanked out. I don't remember everything. My body was no longer my own.

He finally fell asleep, but I did not. I heard Dad's footsteps walking up the stairs to adjust the thermostat. My heart pounded in my head when I heard him open my door. As usual, my dad was making his nightly rounds, quietly checking to be sure we were all safe in our beds.

I could see the horror in his eyes as he realized Hunt was in my bed. In his anger, Dad grabbed him and lifted him up out of the room. He growled, "What are you doing in here?!"

I overheard them fighting. Then, I heard my dad ask him, "Have you been smoking pot?"

Then, there was pushing, pulling, and swinging of hands. Daddy yelled one last time, "Get out of our house!"

Dad went into Aaron's room, next to mine, and closed the door. I could hear their deep voices and almost every word. I heard Dad say, "I could have you both sent to jail. What were you thinking? You know better. He was in Faith's room! He's never allowed in this house ever again. I don't want you around him. You're grounded. Give me your keys and your phone."

I held my knees in a ball, buried my head close to my chest, and tightly closed my eyes. I wanted to make some sense of it all. *Did I do something wrong?*

Then, Daddy came back to my room, and he asked me, "Faith, honey, are you okay? Did he hurt you?"

I didn't want Daddy to be any more angry than he already was, so I lied, "I'm fine."

I didn't want him to leave me. I needed a hug and someone to cry with me. But there I was, alone in my room. Everyone went back to their corners of the house.

What if he comes back? I should have told Dad the truth, but I didn't know what to say.

I rushed to lock my bedroom door, my heart pounding with fear. I wanted to sneak out and run away across the street to Dezzie's house, but instead, I sought refuge in my closet. The questions swirled in my mind, tormenting me: *Should I have yelled out? Should I have fought back? What if he would have hurt me?* These thoughts weighed heavily on me in the silent darkness of the closet.

At that moment, I resolved, *If it ever happens again, I will fight. I will hit him. I will kick. Then, I'll run. I'll go get Daddy immediately.* It was a promise I made to myself, determined to protect myself from any future harm. Then I declared one more promise to myself, *I am my own protector. I will defend myself and others at all costs.* I repeated what I heard Dad say when he swears new recruits into the force.

My thoughts were interrupted by a tap at my window. I didn't want to look. If it was Hunt, I wouldn't know what to do. I shrunk back even further in my closet. There was another light tapping at the window and a girl's voice whispering, "Faith, open the window."

I cautiously opened the curtain and, as my eyes adjusted to the light, I saw Dezzie. Tears streamed down her cheeks. I opened my window, crawled out, and we embraced tightly, both of us sobbing as we sought comfort in one another's presence.

"How did you know I needed you?" I asked Dezzie, still bewildered by her timely arrival.

Tears streamed down her face as she replied, her voice trembling with fear, "What if I lose her, Faith? I don't know what I'll do if I lose her."

Confusion and concern washed over me. "Lose who, Dezzie? Who are you going to lose?"

She could barely speak through her sobs, "Bianca passed out in the driveway. Mom and Dad just rushed her to the hospital. They sent me over here. I don't want to be an only child, Faith. What will I do if my only sister dies?"

Dezzie cried a loud cry. I cried with her. I had nothing to offer except my presence.

"Dezzie, let's go to the treehouse so we don't wake anyone up." We needed a quiet place to cry together. In silence, we made our way up to the treehouse in the darkness, hoping to avoid drawing any attention from our family. Once we were inside, we sat on the bean bags with our blankets and cried. Even after there were no more tears, we just sat quietly. I thought about my dream just a couple of hours earlier. I looked to see if Old Solomon's face moved, but it didn't.

I grabbed a notebook and pen off the bookshelf and journaled all I could remember about my dream. When I looked up at Old Solomon again, I saw something shining in the moonlight. There was liquid under his scars. I reached out and swiped my finger underneath the markings and then tasted it. It tasted salty.

Dezzie asked, "What are you doing?"

"I had another dream tonight," I began, my voice barely above a whisper. "Old Solomon warned me about things to come. He cautioned me to stay strong even when I'm hurting. His last three words were, 'Never lose hope.'"

I proceeded to share everything that Solomon told me during our conversation, explaining the remarkable capacity for both trees and humans to heal after enduring hardships.

"He's nine hundred years old, Dezzie," I continued, emphasizing the incredible wisdom Old Solomon had accumulated over his long life. "He told me to never lose hope. Even in our moments of hurt, because they have purpose and ultimately make us better people. He said that the difficult parts of life have meaning and contribute to our strength. I don't understand it, but I believe him."

I told her that Old Solomon told me to utilize my resources to heal quickly. "He said that our suffering could become a threat if we don't harness it to make us stronger," I said with conviction. "I may not fully understand everything he told me about bitter roots and broken branches, but I do understand that we need to stand together and support each other when we face hard times. He said that we can't grow visual branches like trees can. Our growth happens in our hearts and in our minds. When we are hurting, like we are now, we must heal. We need each other now more than ever. We can't let this stop us from growing into our purpose."

"Faith, if I tell you something, can you promise not to tell anyone?" Dezzie's voice was filled with urgency.

"Of course, Dezzie, you know you can trust me. We share everything," I assured her.

Dezzie hesitated for a moment before continuing, "You know how private Mom and Dad are. It's crucial that it stays between us."

"Pinky swear," I affirmed, and we locked pinky fingers, sealing our promise.

Then, she revealed the painful truth, her voice trembling, "Bianca didn't just pass out in the driveway. She inhaled something that caused her lungs to collapse. She knows she can't smoke or vape with cystic fibrosis. Mom woke me up crying and said they had to leave immediately to get her to the emergency room. I didn't even get to say goodbye to her. Dang it! Why are teenagers so selfish? She knows she can't smoke. Mom has warned her of the dangers of inhaling chemicals in her sick lungs. Will you pray with me that she survives?"

Without hesitation, we joined hands and nodded solemnly. Together, we closed our eyes and prayed for Bianca's recovery, sharing the weight of the moment in silent communion.

I took a deep breath, knowing I had to share my own heavy burden. "Dezzie, there's something I have to tell you too. But you have to promise me you won't tell anyone. Will you promise?"

Dezzie replied firmly, "Faith, you know our agreement."

"But I have to hear you say it." With a deep sigh, she assured me, "Yes, Faith, I promise not to tell anyone what you tell me tonight."

Tears welled up in my eyes as I tried to reveal my own painful truth, "I don't know how to tell you this, but when I woke up from talking to Old Solomon in my dream, Aaron, Bianca, and Hunt were outside talking. I could hear other kids too. There was music and laughing. I thought about spying on them, but I knew they wouldn't like it if they found me, so I went back to bed. I stayed awake until I heard cars leaving. I fell back into a heavy sleep. When I woke up," I paused, taking a sobbing breath, "Dezzie, someone else was in my bed."

I couldn't speak. I was nauseated. She wouldn't understand. I just told her that something horrible had happened in my house. I could not stomach fully sharing everything. I tried to explain my sense of fear at hearing her tapping on the window, thinking it might be someone else, and the relief that overcame me seeing her at my window. Her presence had been a lifeline in my moment of need.

We both cried so hard that neither of us could speak for a long time.

Then, I finally mustered the strength to say, "I've got more than a broken arm; I have a broken heart." I spoke through the tears, sobbing, "But you know, Old Solomon did say that trees help one another when they are stressed. He also believes that God created humans to support one another when we are going through tough times, by encouragement and prayer. We must stay strong, not just for ourselves, but for each other, so we don't stop growing."

In an effort to transfer some healing to her, I reached out to her with my good hand on her foot and said, "I'm so sorry about Bianca." My empathy for her and myself overwhelmed me.

I looked down at the floor of the treehouse and started to cry all over again.

"This all stinks," Dezzie echoed with sentiment, her voice heavy with sorrow.

I proposed making a pact between us. I held up my right arm from the shoulder up in the cast, stretching out my fingers in a solemn gesture, committing myself to the promise I was about to make.

"I swear to you, Dezzie, and to the Lord, Jesus Christ, that I will not inhale or take harmful chemicals," I affirmed with unwavering dedication. "I don't ever want to hurt myself or anyone else, especially our parents. Drugs make people do awful things and have sad consequences."

We leaned against Old Solomon's trunk, finding solace in each other's company as we talked and cried, our shared pain drawing us closer together.

Eventually, exhaustion overcame us, and we fell asleep beneath the watchful gaze of the ancient tree. With only a couple hours of sleep, Mrs. Diamond woke us up from our slumber, her voice carrying a hint of desperation as she called out Dezzie's name as if she feared she had gone missing. Slowly, I awoke to the reality of last night. I remembered we were in the treehouse, and I peeked my head out of the door. "Mrs. Diamond, we're up here," I called down to her.

I could see the dread in her weary eyes. In a low monotone voice, drained of energy and emotion, she told us, "Girls, it's time to get up. Dezzie, we have to get ready for church." The Diamond family's commitment to St. Patrick's Catholic Church is unwavering, even in times of tragedy. It seemed that she didn't even mind or care that we spent the night in the treehouse. That night marked the first of many overnights in the Bright Light Treehouse with Old Solomon.

I grabbed the treehouse journal to take with me. Returning home, I climbed back through my opened window. My door remained locked from the inside. I didn't usually bathe in the morning, but I did that day. I jumped from my room to the bathroom before anyone else woke up. Within a few minutes, Oliver yelled outside the bathroom door, "What's taking you so long? Get out! It's my turn."

I wrapped my towel around my head and another around my body, ran to my room, and locked the door. I stayed in my room getting ready and wasting time for as long as I could.

I journaled. I wrote as much as I could remember. "Never lose hope" were the last three words I heard. The house got quiet when the family finally left to load up the van. I prayed they would just go on to church without me. "Faith, honey, we have to go." Daddy talked to me from the other side of the closed door. "I'm serving communion today, and I need to be there a little early."

I didn't feel like going anywhere that morning. I sat there, reflecting on the wisdom Old Solomon had shared with me in my dream. A branch has been cut off, and I was no longer innocent to the hurt of someone I love. But just as Old Solomon could heal, so could I. I knew I had to start healing quickly, utilizing the resources available to me. Allowing this pain to fester could be detrimental, and I needed to work hard to be the person God plans for me to be. In a quiet prayer, I pleaded, "Lord, help me."

CHAPTER 12

FAITH BEGINS TO HEAL

Throughout the entire ride to church, I found myself engaged in a silent dialogue with unfamiliar voices inside my head. As my parents debated over the amount to write for the tithe check, one of these voices told me that we were poor. It was a thought that had never crossed my mind before. My dad always quipped that we were rich in love, and that's all that mattered. Then, I heard my brothers lamenting about how exhausted they were and how they would rather be at home sleeping. Sundays had always been our favorite day as a family, or so I thought. And then there was me, grappling with my own sour mood. I wondered why today, the Lord's day, was so heavy and laden with negativity. It felt out of place from our family's usual harmony. I frowned and gazed at the trees as we drove past, ignoring the silence. I couldn't muster a smile or the energy to chime in as I carried the heavy burden that no child should have to bear alone. My family needed a rescue, a way to shake off this oppressive mood. A haunting thought crossed my mind, "What if this is the beginning of the end? I may wither away from within as Old Solomon said some people do." The ride to church seemed longer than usual. When we finally pulled into the parking lot, we all separated into our own spaces without saying a word. The only sound I heard were the whispers of the voices taunting me.

Sunday School class was a much-needed distraction. My friends looked radiant in their freshly rolled waterfall ringlets and flowing dresses. Then, the voices appeared again. I noticed details that I never noticed before. Small irritations like my half-painted fingernails and cheap lip gloss stirred something inside that told me I was less important than the other girls in the classroom, saying, "You don't look as pretty as they do."

I concealed my inner turmoil beneath a facade of false cheer, pretending to be happy. With a half-hearted smile masking my deep-seated fear, I dreaded the unwelcome transformation within myself. Any hint of sadness might attract unwanted attention. Above all, I cringed at the thought of my teacher questioning my dad about my melancholy demeanor in Sunday School. Seated on the front row, I wrestled with the sensation that I was spiraling into madness. I just might slip out of class to go to the restroom if these voices got any louder. The Sunday School class began with the strains of two hymns, accompanied by the aged piano that rang out off-key, and the recitation of the Lord's Prayer. Then, Mr. Acres, the elder in charge of our class, made an important announcement, requesting everyone's undivided attention.

Our pastor entered the room, and a hush fell over the class. All eyes were on him as he greeted us with a warm smile. "Good morning, children," he began. "I want to invite you to join me every Thursday after school for a special class where we will learn the Shorter Catechism. This will be a weekly commitment where we will be memorizing questions and answers related to your beliefs. In this class, you will gain a foundational understanding of God, baptism, the Lord's Prayer, Communion, and more. Please discuss this with your parents to arrange transportation, and make sure you arrive on time. We'll also provide snacks and juice at every meeting. I hope to see you there." The pastor's announcement caught my attention, offering a potential resource that would be a valuable part of my healing journey.

As our Sunday School teacher opened the class for prayer requests, I found myself raising my hand, an uncommon occurrence for me. He called on me, asking, "Faith, how can we pray for you?"

"Please pray for my broken branch, I mean, my broken arm. Please pray for healing for my broken arm." Inadvertently, "broken branch" had slipped out. I realized that my recent conversation with Old Solomon had been on my mind so much that it had resurfaced in my request without me even consciously thinking about it.

After he prayed for everyone's requests, our teacher shifted the topic to baptism, saying, "Most of you born into this church were baptized as infants. Your parents have probably shown you pictures or told you about that glorious day. For you and your family, it was a public profession of belief in God and His promises. God keeps His promises and we acknowledge that, as your parents and your elders, we believe that you are a child of God and included in that promise. We commit to teaching you about God. Today, we're going to shift our focus from your baptism to Jesus' baptism. Did you know Jesus was baptized too?"

"Why would Jesus need to be baptized? He is already God," came a voice from the back of the room.

He answered, "Many of the high priests who questioned Jesus as the true Son of God were standing there watching John baptize Jesus when God spoke from Heaven saying, 'This is my Son in whom I am well pleased.' They knew about the prophecy of Isaiah and Joel and of the Holy Spirit being 'poured' out like water to cleanse and purify those who followed Jesus. And yet, they still denied that Jesus was the Messiah whom the prophets of old spoke about."

My ears perked up when he said, "cleanse and purify." *I am dirty*, I admitted silently, feeling unworthy and tainted by impurity. All I yearned for was that sense of cleansing and purification. Then, a thought struck me like never before: *You're not like the other children.* A sea of self-doubt washed over me. Staring at my polished shoes, a sense of shame washed over me. The ruffled lace on my dress and the curls in my hair were pretty, but I didn't feel pretty. Maybe I was too focused on fitting in outwardly, but deep down, I knew I was different from all the other children. This internal struggle was new, and I despised it. For the first time in my life, I felt like an outsider, as if I didn't belong.

With my hand up, I blurted out, "Is the water magic?" I asked. "Like, does the water automatically make you feel clean? I mean, does it make people pure again?"

"Faith, thank you for asking. That's a common misunderstanding, and I want to make it clear that baptism tells the story of our rescue from sin by Jesus through faith in His death and resurrection. Baptism in the Presbyterian church is a sign and a seal of the covenant of grace made by God through Jesus and extended to us. It's an act of obedience for parents and the members in the church to pledge to raise you to know who Christ is and to be a good witness of Christ to you. It's not about feelings, Faith. It is the Holy Spirit who gives you the power to overcome your feelings and rest in the saving grace of Jesus," he answered me.

That wasn't the answer I needed, but I was willing to take a chance. I knew I needed the power of the Holy Spirit, so I asked him, "Can we do that today? I'm ready. Please, I really need to be baptized today. I wasn't baptized as a baby like everyone else in here. It's a confusing story, but my dad was raised Baptist. He was dunked. He likes everything about the Presbyterian church except infant baptism. He wants us to be sprinkled when we're ready. Is that okay?"

"Faith, I like your enthusiasm. Let's talk after class. We schedule baptisms weeks in advance. You'll meet with Pastor Journey so he can pray with you."

His interpretation of my enthusiasm was actually desperation. He had no idea how serious I was. That was not what I wanted to hear, but I didn't dare argue with the elder.

"Yes, sir," I said. At least there was hope for the healing to begin. I was already feeling a bit better about my broken branch.

After the lesson was concluded, my teacher asked if anyone wanted to be baptized. I raised my hand just in case he forgot. If I was going to have secrets that deep and strange voices in my head, I knew I needed God's help.

I don't know what the sermon was about or what the preacher said in church that day, but I know what I said in my heart. I prayed long and earnestly for Jesus to be the source of healing for my broken branches. I thanked Him for giving me a daddy that brings us to church even on the days we don't feel like coming. I took out my journal and sketched a picture of Old Solomon, the treehouse, the swings, and the signs above the door. The symbols of the cross, triangle, and the heart represented our family motto: "Jesus changes hearts." As I drew them, a sense of awe filled my chest, sending shivers down my arms. I traced those symbols all around Old Solomon, repeating the motto in my mind. It was no longer just a picture or a mission to be accomplished; it became my life, a reminder that only Jesus can change my heart. He was at work, molding me into the person He wanted me to be. I was leaving behind a childish faith, but the new Faith that was emerging within me would be even stronger.

On the way home, when Daddy asked us if we learned anything new in church, I told everyone in the van what we learned in Sunday School. I said, "I'm getting baptized, and I want to sign up for the Catechism Class on Thursday afternoons."

Mom responded first, "Faith, that is an answer to my prayers and makes me so happy. Now we're both family on earth and in Heaven."

After lunch, I walked to Dezzie's house, and before I could knock, Dezzie opened the door. "I've been standing here watching your house from the window. Come on in. Mom and Dad are at the hospital, and I hate being alone."

The usual tranquil atmosphere was replaced by tension. There were no cookies and milk waiting on the kitchen counter as usual, and the Diamond home was filled with an eerie silence.

"How's Bianca feeling today?" I asked.

"Oh Faith, it's horrible. They said that both of Bianca's lungs collapsed and that she may not live," she cried.

I cried with her. I had no idea it was that serious. We are both dealing with so much loss and heartache. We just sat quietly for a long time. I finally spoke up, "Dezzie, I feel like I'm going stir crazy in my head. I'm thinking things that I've never thought before, and I don't feel like myself anymore. I've made up my mind to follow Old Solomon's advice and use all my resources to heal. I'm getting baptized."

Dezzie, looking up from her despair, seemed relieved and mustered the ability to speak, saying, "Really?"

"Yes, Dezzie, I'll do anything to get these voices out of my head. This morning was so weird. In the car on the ride to church, Mom and Dad argued about money. Then, the boys were fussy, complaining that they didn't want to go to church. I didn't feel like going to church either, but I didn't dare say so. It all seemed so sad. Then, when I walked in church, I felt like I didn't quite belong. Dezzie, I've been in that church my whole life. I love that place. But today, it was like a dark cloud was looming over me. Remember the old cartoons that Mom talks about with the angel on one shoulder and the devil on the other? That's what it was like. I couldn't concentrate on Sunday School because the voices in my head were louder than the teacher. I was suddenly aware of details that I had never noticed before. Then, out of the blue, the elder explained baptism, and he said the words, 'cleansing and purifying.' When I heard those two words, I knew there was hope for me. Mom is right. We need a purification of the heart and mind. Dezzie, we need Jesus now more than ever."

"I was actually going to tell you a couple of weeks ago, but after finishing our treehouse and your broken arm, I forgot. I start Confirmation Class next week."

"Oh Dezzie, that's great," I was relieved.

She went on to tell me about how her church requires classes. They were similar but different from my church. The idea was the same, Jesus saves. They wanted us to know what we were getting ourselves into when we dedicate our lives to following Him. It was good to get our minds off of Bianca and on to hope for our future. We didn't know what tomorrow was going to bring, but we knew that, with God's help, we would somehow be okay. Neither Bianca's sickness nor my awful situation were going to define us. We agreed that the church and the truths we were learning were helping us. She had a desire to know more and to get answers to all of her questions. And I needed faith to know that I could trust what I could not see.

Dezzie's parents drove up, so I gave her a hug and told her to call me if she needed me. I went home so they could be alone as a family.

Flash Forward, How's Hope?

Hope interrupted Faith, asking, "Faith, can I ask you a question? Do you have to be a member of a church to be baptized?"

I answered, "No, Hope, you don't. We can baptize you in the chapel.

"I would like that," She stated.

It was the most calm and sure statement she made in our meeting that day. I was grateful she was listening. I still had so much to share with her.

"Faith, thank you for sharing your story. I forget how much I enjoy having a friend to talk to. I've never known anyone else who could relate to me like you can. I don't feel so alone. In a weird sort of way, hearing your story makes me feel better."

"Yes, I know how you feel. Safety comes in knowing others and being known and loved for who you are. Freedom comes with being real with others, holding nothing back. Revealing secrets releases the shame and worry that we associate with those secrets. We feel lighter. Jesus wants to take our load. He will carry it for you. You no longer have to. You may not feel free to share all your secrets yet, but give it time. What you will find here at the Bright Light Safe House is a safe sisterhood. These girls are all learning to open up and share in the safety of small groups. Little by little, it gets easier. You all are more alike than different."

"You seem very comfortable talking to me about your past. I'm sorry I interrupted. Please tell me, what happened next?" Hope asked.

CHAPTER 13

DEZZIE'S LOSS

Flashback to Faith as a Child
The Next Day:

A knock at my window. "Faith," she barely spoke my name. I opened the window. Dezzie's face was red. Her eyes were red from crying. "Bianca died. She's gone, Faith. I'm an only child."

We walked to the treehouse in complete silence. I looked at the sign outside of the entrance: "The Bright Light Treehouse: Daddy's Angels Headquarters, Det. Faith Joule and Det. Dezzie Diamond." I touched it, remembering our creed that now seemed paradoxical. I was crushed under the weight of despair for my friend, remembering our promise to each other "to confront danger head-on while others shy away from it." Our mission, once fueled by what seemed like supernatural strength, had vanished. It all felt like child's play now. I couldn't help but ask myself, "Were we shielded by a force stronger than ourselves?"

At that moment, we were anything but strong. There we sat in the treehouse. Cradled by the sturdy branches, we were held by Old Solomon's embrace. It became our safe haven, our refuge for finding hope. How I longed to rewind time, to possess the wisdom I now held, to avert this turmoil altogether. If only I knew then what I knew now, I could have prevented all of this mess. As I reflected on our once lofty ambitions as "Daddy's Angels," I pondered our newfound responsibilities: feeding puppies, babysitting Paul, and gardening for Mr. O'Conner. How would we continue in our quest to help those who depended on us most?

An unwelcome thought occurred to me for the first time. "You're a loser," the voices whispered once more, persuading me to surrender. After all, I was certainly no "Daddy's Angel". I felt more like Daddy's fallen angel. I looked out of the treehouse window. The corner of my house peeked out from around the trees on the other side of the street. Looking at the back patio of Dezzie's home, the expanse of the yard, and the pond, the memories of our childhood were now just that, memories. No matter how I tried to hold on to my youth, it was now behind me. Unlike my broken arm, there was no brace to put our broken hearts back together again. The questions flooded my mind, "Why us? Why now?"

There was a knock on the treehouse door and a voice asking, "Girls, are you in there?"

"Yes," I walked to the door. "Who is it?"

The voice was familiar, but I couldn't place it.

"It's me, Grace, your new youth minister from church."

I opened the door, initially taken aback by her unexpected appearance.

Relieved to see her, I wanted to fall into her arms and get some kind of reassurance. But she wasn't there for me. She was there for Dezzie. She walked past me.

"See? I told you. You're a loser," the voices mocked me.

"Dezzie," she said, walking over to hug her. "I'm so sorry about your sister."

We barely knew Grace, but we had quickly grown to admire her after our first purity class. She was the ideal comforter and had gained Dezzie's appreciation after she told her she was a 'diamond in God's eyes' at the initial meeting. She embodied the essence of comfort—a youthful woman not bound by blood but genuinely concerned for our well-being.

"Faith, your mom called me and asked me to come sit with you girls while she helps Mrs. Diamond with plans for the funeral," she spoke softly.

It made sense that Mom orchestrated her arrival. After all, Mom trusted Grace as a leader for us. To our surprise, Grace disclosed that she had a sister that passed away when she was a teenager. In the most comforting tone, careful not to discount Dezzie's feelings, Grace said, "Dezzie, I was in your shoes when I was your age. I truly know how you feel. My sister died in a car wreck," she shared. "It was difficult growing up without her, but not impossible."

Her genuine sympathy was palpable, and we sensed that she truly could empathize with Dezzie's sorrow. Dezzie, rendered speechless, gave Grace a pleasant nod, letting her know that she heard and appreciated her.

Grace then turned her attention to me and, looking at me with pleasant eyes, she said, "Faith, I'm so glad Dezzie has you as a trusted friend. Can I give you some advice that I've learned over the years as I've walked through this pain with my friends and family who have lost a loved one?"

"Sure," I said. I couldn't imagine what she was about to say, but I needed direction.

"She needs you now more than ever. Let her cry, even when you least expect it. Listen without interrupting when she voices her sadness or confusion, and encourage her the best you know how. Grief has multiple layers. There are times when she may be angry. Just listen. You don't have to have all the answers. Your presence is sometimes all that she'll need. You will be her loving space to land when her swirling thoughts start to spiral, so your kindness during this time will mean the world to her. You two are very blessed to have one another."

"She can count on me," I assured her.

"I'm so glad to hear you say that. As hard as it may be, Dezzie needs to get up and get outside every day. Keep working on your missions. Your mom told me about your new Daddy's Angels service. In a strange sort of way, helping others is very helpful in helping ourselves."

"Really? You think?" I asked.

"Yes, when we help others who are struggling, we are reminded that we aren't alone. Everyone is experiencing something difficult, Faith. It's part of the human experience. When we work together to solve a problem, we realize we need others to get through it together."

Dezzie had been quiet until that point. Then she said, "There's no way it will ever be the same without Bianca. Every decision our family made revolved around her illness. She's the reason we homeschooled. Don't you see? That's why I think about the safety of everything, Faith. Now what? If something happens to me, then my parents have no children left. I have to be extra careful."

Realizing she admitted a fear that she never allowed herself to say aloud, she apologized. "I'm sorry. I shouldn't have said that.

Bianca couldn't help that she was born with cystic fibrosis. It wasn't her fault."

A moment of silence hung in the air to let those heavy words settle. Grace gently reassured Dezzie, "When my sister died, I felt very alone, like no one understood what I was going through. Healing your broken heart takes time. It's a complex process. Remembering her and speaking positively about her will help. Your family will always have an empty seat at the table where Bianca used to sit. Honoring her and remembering her well will help you to grieve. You will celebrate her birthday and grieve today's date of her passing. But don't lose hope. You will move forward and find joy in life again.

I looked at Grace and at Dezzie, "Don't lose hope." I repeated. There are those three words again. I looked up at Old Solomon. I looked at Grace. I looked at Dezzie. "Never lose hope," I said with a hushed voice. I needed that reminder as much as Dezzie did.

Grace became our mentor, showing up each consecutive day of the week of Bianca's funeral. I don't know if our moms asked her to or if she volunteered to help us, but we loved having her around to persuade us to keep moving forward. Whatever we were up to, she followed along. Whether we were feeding puppies, babysitting Paul, or even working in Mr. O'Conner's flower beds, Grace gave us permission to grieve by quietly living life beside us. One day, she even challenged us to run with her.

"We run the bases at softball, but running any other distance just for sport seems so boring."

"The best runs are shared with friends," she said. "We could go on a short jog. Come on, you can do it."

Dezzie was having a hard day and didn't feel like going with us. Bianca's funeral was the next day, and she was very sad.

"I just need to be alone for a few minutes," Dezzie admitted. "You two go on without me."

Grace nodded and looked at me, saying, "It's okay, let her go home. It's important that we don't push her. She might join us in the future, but today, let her rest."

We stretched for a few minutes, and then we walked.

She told me, "Faith, if you're going to become a runner, there are a few things you should know. We're going to start out walking fast to warm up our muscles. Then, we'll jog. We may repeat the walk and jog several times today, and the next few times, we run. We'll increase our running time each run. Once you get over the initial lung-crushing, muscle-aching first few runs, you learn to enjoy it, like a new hobby. As it is with other self-disciplines, you have to push through the hard parts and keep going, even when your body thinks it wants to quit."

"You said running is a hobby and a self-discipline. How can running be both fun and hard?" I asked.

"Well, as I said, if you can get through the battle of the body versus the mind, you'll earn the opportunity to enjoy it. No matter what new thing you pursue in life, there's always a struggle before the win. Once your body gets accustomed to the endurance, you won't be distracted by the thought of running, but, instead, you'll crave the benefits."

"There are benefits to running?" I asked.

"Yes, for sure. Physically, you'll maintain your weight by burning calories, and strengthen your muscles, heart, and lungs. More importantly, you'll improve your mental health as you gain confidence and look back at your accomplishments. It's proven by research that running improves your energy too. So, since you're doing your body a favor, you'll want to reward yourself and celebrate every time you finish a run. Don't go crazy, but treat yourself with something that relaxes you. For me, it's a hot shower or, if I have time, a long bath. I have some great recipes for some yummy healthy smoothies. Whatever it is, give yourself something to look forward to. Even your rewards can have healthy benefits."

She sounded very wise, like Old Solomon. I realized that running was another resource that I could use to help myself heal from the inside out. I was convinced that this was a good hobby for me.

"What are we waiting for? Let's run," I said.

Within a few blocks, I was struggling to breathe and suffering from side stitches. I had to walk. That first day was rough, but Grace didn't give up on me. As I stood bent over, holding my sides, she spoke wise words over me.

"Remember, Faith, take a break if you need to, catch your breath, and then push through the struggle. Rest is just around the corner. This chapter in your life is like running. It's the first time you or Dezzie have grieved loss. Keep showing up for yourself and your family, especially your friend, Dezzie, and I promise, it does get easier."

"Grace, can you keep a secret? I could never tell Dezzie this." I hesitated, and then I said, "I don't want to go to the funeral." I looked away, ashamed that I said it out loud.

"It's not because I don't want to be there for Dezzie, but I'm so sad for her that I don't want any more sadness. Can I skip it? I mean, I have never been to a funeral, and I don't know what to expect. I'm a little scared. I can stay at her house with some of the other ladies from her church and prepare lunch. I would prefer to stay here," I admitted.

"Faith, you have to be at the church for Dezzie. She needs to see you there supporting her and her parents. You will be there. If I have to come get you myself, you will go."

"But what do I say or do there that I can't say or do here?" I asked.

"It's not about what you say or do, Faith. Your mere presence will reassure her. It's the most important thing you can do. Show up," she said with one hand on my shoulder.

The next day, Grace called my mom to be sure that I was going to the funeral. Mom reassured her that I was going. My family arrived early and sat quietly up close to the front of the sanctuary. Grace sat with us. The priest delivered a short sermon about children entering Heaven. He began by addressing the family, looking at Mr. and Mr. Diamond. He quoted Psalm 42:11, "'Why, my soul, are you downcast? Why so disturbed within me? Put your hope in God, for I will yet praise him, my Savior and my God.' Today, we will remember Bianca with sadness for us who are here on earth and we will hold on to hope until we join her in Heaven."

Then, he looked at Dezzie and up at all of us, saying, "Be assured that Bianca is in Heaven with Jesus. He loves and honors children who seek after Him. Jesus told the disciples that they are to be like the children who follow and trust Him. Children are considered to be the greatest in the kingdom of Heaven."

I've seen paintings of Jesus and children all around him in the nursery at church. I thought that was just an artist's rendering for the sake of the nursery. He referenced Jesus's teaching from Matthew 18, recounting the disciples' inquiry about greatness in the kingdom of Heaven. Jesus responded by having a young child stand beside him, highlighting the significance of childlike trust. As I listened, a feeling of importance swelled within me. "Matthew 18," I murmured to myself. "I'll read that again at home."

As soon as we got home from the funeral, I ran to my room and opened my Bible to Matthew 18. I read through verses one to five a couple of times. I read verse four again, "Therefore, whoever takes the lowly position of this child is the greatest in the kingdom of Heaven." Lowly versus greatest were two opposing ideas presented together. We'd been studying chiastic structure in Sunday

School. Chiastic Structure is two big words that mean opposing thoughts presented together. For example, "The first shall be last and the last shall be first." Jesus likes chiastic structure. After all, He was the greatest in the kingdom of Heaven and came down to earth, born in a lowly stable. He was saying to the disciples, "I am not asking you to do anything that I haven't done." He was a humble example and of one who was exalted.

I sensed the Holy Spirit nudge me to continue reading, guiding me through verse six and on to verse seven. "If anyone causes one of these little ones–those who believe in me–to stumble, it would be better for them to have a large millstone hung around their neck and to be drowned in the depths of the sea. Woe to the world because of the things that cause people to stumble! Such things must come, but woe to the person through whom they come."

In that moment, I felt as though a gavel struck in my mind, affirming my worth. That marked the beginning of my healing journey. The burden of guilt lifted, and the shame began to dissolve. I realized that Jesus understood exactly what I was going through, and he placed those verses in the Bible for me that very day. Encouraged and validated, I knew I needed to step out of my room. So, I laced up my shoes and went for a run around the block.

Over the course of several weeks, running became increasingly manageable for me. Often, when I struggled to speak because I was out of breath, Grace effortlessly filled the silence with stories from her childhood. She shared her own aspirations to help others, revealing that we had more in common than I had realized. Beyond serving as a mentor and a valuable resource, Grace became a trusted friend.

I noticed a clarity in my mind, and surprisingly, I found myself running more for the sheer joy of it rather than solely for sport. Exploring the open road became a form of therapy for me. When I shared my experience with Grace, she shed light on the phenomenon known as the "runner's high." This natural high is attributed to the release of certain hormones during intense exercise, as well as new blood vessels that nourish our brain, collectively contributing to an uplifted mood.

"Grace, remember when you told me how important it was for me to support Dezzie as she grieved? And how staying busy would help her to keep moving forward?"

"Yes, you're such a good friend to her," Grace assured me.

"Instead of running across the street to talk to her first thing each day, I have been running around the block instead. It works. After a run, I'm not as talkative when I do go to her house. Running, walking, and talking to Jesus has been good for me. It helps me to get my energy out so I'm a better friend and listener. Thank you for taking the time to teach me about running. It's helped me in so many ways."

Grace smiled, saying, "You're welcome."

Grace may not have fully grasped the depths of what I was going through, but she didn't need to. She recognized that girls my age struggle with physical, mental, and spiritual growth because she once walked in those same shoes.

"I'm still hearing some voices that try to bring me down, but I hear them less when I'm running."

"What do they say?"

"They tell me I'm a loser. They tell me I'm different."

"My youth pastor once told me, 'Someone who lives in the past has no future.' You and Dezzie must keep putting one foot in front of the other, always moving forward one step at a time," Grace said.

The idea of forging ahead without any answers, without closure, without even a sliver of acknowledgment, accepting that the most traumatic event in my life will never be addressed, sent my heart racing with palpitations. A knot twisted in my stomach, crept up to my chest, and constricted my throat– an emotional trigger pulled.

Tears welled up in my eyes, and I poured out, "One minute I seem fine, the next I'm falling apart. There are moments I want to scream in frustration. It's like there's a storm raging in my chest that I can't contain. I know anger is not acceptable as a Christian, but I simply can't make it go away on my own. Sometimes I retreat to my room to muffle my screams into my pillow or I clench a towel between my teeth to avoid an outburst. Then, I go for a run. It's so nice to get outside."

Grace seemed confused, so she asked, "Faith, has something happened that I don't know about?"

I told her everything about that night.

She didn't seem surprised but instead asked me, "Do your parents know?"

"Yes, my dad does. I assumed he told my mom, but we never talked about it. I think it would make us all feel uncomfortable. I would rather not bring it up with them." I said.

"We can make an appointment to sit down and talk if that would make you feel better," she offered. "Faith, I have a book I want you to read this week. I have a few in my car. It's from an author who had a very similar experience. She is now a counselor and helps girls like you. I think you'll relate to her and her story."

"I'm not the only person?" I asked. "There's a book written about this?" I asked before she could answer my first question. I was shocked. Relieved and, yet, sad on a whole new level, grieving for myself and for other children who are like me.

"Yes, Faith, sadly, it happens more than any of us would like to admit. It's as many as one in three girls who have experienced sexual abuse. Consider a room of twelve girls. It's possible that four of them have experienced some sort of sexual misconduct. Healing early is important. In this book, you'll learn how other women have been able to get over their past and move forward. I want you to read a chapter a day and we'll talk about it on our runs."

I took that book home, and I read three chapters before I fell asleep. I was on a mission to keep moving forward no matter what tried to hold me back. Every time I thought about the past, I repeated these words to myself, 'Someone who lives in the past has no future.'

CHAPTER 14

JESUS CHANGES FAITH'S HEART

Two Months later:

I found myself immersed in a remarkably vivid dream, one where I was soaring above my yard as if I were a drone. The sensation of control was tangible as I steered through the skies, yet the realization of possessing such power to traverse the heights was utterly surprising. The dream materialized with me, already airborne, suspended over Old Solomon and the treehouse. Hovering in the sky, I relished the liberty of surveying his crown, the feeling of freedom coursing through me. However, this reverie was gently interrupted by the morning sun's radiance, filtering through partially drawn blinds and casting a spotlight upon my bed. In that moment, the celestial flight ceased, but my yearning to return to those weightless skies remained fervent. With a sense of determination, I shut my eyes, attempting to recapture the euphoric sensation akin to an eagle gracefully navigating the open expanse of air. My mind tried to fly once again, but my stomach growled, reminding me that I'm not in Heaven yet.

A mouth-watering aroma of seared meat awoke my senses. Up to my feet, one foot in front of the other, I shuffled to the kitchen for Sunday morning breakfast. My parents spoke softly as dishes and coffee cups danced around the countertops. My bare feet softly stepped in, and without saying a word, I climbed into Mom's lap for snuggles.

As Daddy stirred the eggs, he said, "Today is the big day, Faith. Are you ready for your baptism?"

I imagined myself standing by the baptismal font in front of the sunlit sanctuary as the rays streamed in the stained glass windows. In my sleepy stupor, I remembered with a smile my most adored pink and white dress with lace around the sleeves and shiny buttons up the neck.

I hesitated to ask Mom about the dress because I know how precious weekend mornings are to her as she sips her cup of coffee. Mom abides by a certain rule: "Anticipate tomorrow today. If you neglect to prepare, don't expect me to step in." In other words, she isn't fond of eleventh-hour preparations. Nonetheless, given her bustling schedule and work commitments, she is not always able to plan in advance. So we broach our clothes in a tactful manner. We do help, but Mom possesses an innate awareness and ability to locate our stuff that escapes us.

As I sidestepped the fact that I had not adhered to the "plan ahead" principle, I inquired, "Mom, by any chance, have you come across my pink and white dress?"

Her lips pushed over to one side of her face, and she raised one eyebrow as her eyes looked off into the distance.

Before she could answer, a misty image of my dress gradually sharpened into focus. Within seconds, I pictured my favorite dress, the only dress I yearned to wear for my baptism, hanging in the laundry room, the neighbor's laundry room. A surge of exhilaration pulsed through me, my heart racing in response.

"Nevermind Mom, I know where it is."

That dress consumed my thoughts entirely, dominating my consciousness. In a matter of seconds, I was fully awake. The oven's timer beeped, acting as an added jolt, electrifying my nerves. One singular mission dominated my mind, "I must retrieve that dress."

I dashed to my room, compelled to check my closet, entertaining the notion that perhaps my mind was tricking me. I took a quick glance right to left, brushing my hand across my hanging clothes, but the dress was not in my closet.

"Daddy's Angel to the rescue!" I thought.

I sprinted out of the front door, still in my nightgown, and ran across the street. The Diamonds' family car was gone. I knocked on the door anyway. Recognizing their absence, I checked the doors to confirm they were locked. The side gate was unlocked, allowing me easy access to the backyard. I pulled a lawn chair over, carefully lifted the window, climbed in, and grabbed the dress hanging on the rack beside the dryer. Back through the window, I climbed. I put the lawn chair back on the patio where it belonged. I walked back through the gate, being sure to close it securely, and zipped back across the street to my house.

I stood in front of mom, and I held it up as if it were a victor's trophy. "Do you remember? Dezzie borrowed it for her confirmation last month."

"Faith, I'm disappointed that you went into their laundry room uninvited. Next time, let's think ahead. Now, will you plug in the hot rollers? We need to get ready," Mom said.

I was in the family room buckling my shoes, announcing to any ears who would listen, "I'm almost ready." My parents stepped into the room. Dad handed me a little box wrapped in white paper with a white bow. "For me?" I asked as I opened the box. We have a tradition in our home. When my brothers and sister were baptized, they were given a piece of jewelry with our family's motto. Aaron and Oliver got leather bracelets with a gold piece sewn in the middle. Joy has a necklace. I opened the box. A shiny gold chain with 3 charms, a cross, a triangle, and a heart. My first real piece of jewelry.

Dad walked behind me, placed it around my neck, and fastened the clip.

He said, "Jesus changes hearts, Faith. Jesus is working to change your heart too. I'm so grateful that you've accepted Jesus and put your trust in Him."

My parents' motto, "Jesus changes hearts" is our family's mission statement that was decided years before I was born. Jesus changing hearts is not written with words but with symbols that are represented by the cross, the triangle and the heart. I looked in the mirror, and staring back at me was a girl becoming a woman before my eyes. This wasn't a homemade yarn necklace with edible cereal charms. No, this necklace was proof that my parents trusted me to take responsibility for a real piece of fine jewelry.

"All of my children are now walking with Jesus. There's nothing that makes a father more happy," Dad said as he looked up at the ceiling. "They're all Yours, Jesus."

Then the voices started. No one heard them but me as they whispered, "You don't deserve this necklace." The voices were right. I didn't deserve Jesus's forgiveness. That's true for everyone, my pastor says. I didn't deserve any of it. I was not pure. I was no longer an innocent little girl. That's why Jesus came, to save sinners like me.

On the drive to church, I held on to the necklace, reassuring myself it was still there. I was so happy and, yet, so plagued with worry that it might slip away from me. Everything I hold sacred tends to get lost or damaged over time. I didn't want to lose this necklace.

Mom and Dad took me to the Amazing Grace Presbyterian Church library, where Pastor Journey was waiting for us.

"Come on in and have a seat, Faith. Tom, you and Mrs. Joule can go get a seat on the front row. I'll bring Faith in to sit by you just before eleven o'clock."

Mom and Dad closed the door on their way out. There, I sat with the two couples holding their infants. Pastor Journey gave his full attention to me.

"Faith, with the authority given to me as the pastor of this church, I will now confirm your decision. Have you admitted that you are a sinner in need of a savior?"

"Yes, sir, I have."

"Do you believe that Jesus is the Christ, the Son of the living God?"

"Yes, sir, I do."

"Are you willing to change your life to leave the past behind and follow Jesus?"

"Yes sir, I am."

"Repeat after me. Dear Jesus, I believe."

I repeated, "Dear Jesus, I believe."

"That You are the Christ, Son of the living God."

I repeated, "That You are the Christ, Son of the living God."

And he went on through the whole sinner's prayer as I repeated what he said. When we were done, everyone in the room gave me a handshake and a hug.

"Welcome to the family, Faith. Let's walk on into the sanctuary and tell everyone the good news." As we walked, he reminded me, "Faith, I want to remind you that the water in the baptismal has been blessed. There's nothing magical about it. It's a symbol of your new life in Christ. When I ask the questions of the congregation to be a participant in these children's Christian upbringing, you will answer them as well as the congregation. Since you are now an official member of the church, you are joining the faith family. It is all of our responsibility to show the younger generation how to live like Jesus. You'll help lead and guide those under your care.

"Yes, sir," I acknowledged him respectfully.

I followed him through the restricted "Pastoral Staff Only" secret door, through the secret passageway around the back of the sanctuary, to the other secret door that led into the front of the sanctuary where the preacher gives his sermons.

Mom and Dad were sitting in the front row singing my favorite hymn, 'To God be the Glory.' Not only was that my favorite hymn, but it was written by the historically famous Fanny Crosby. I felt like God was giving His nod of approval by including that hymn in today's plan of worship. My Sunday School class studied hymns and their authors. From the late 1800s to the early 1900s, Mrs. Crosby overcame all the odds stacked against her. When she was a baby, she lost her sight from an eye infection. However, thanks to the teaching of her mom and grandmother, she overcame her disability, excelled in music, and attended a music school. In her ninety-four years, she wrote over 8,000 hymns. As a missionary and a lay pastor, she memorized chapters in the Bible, excelled as a student, and was a teacher at the blind school that she attended as a young woman. She even met presidents. Like Old Solomon, she was wise. I prayed, "Lord, help me to be wise."

Singing along with them, I sat beside Mom and Dad. When the last verse of the hymn was over, Pastor Journey told everyone about our meeting in the library. He prepared the congregation for baptism, saying, "Sometimes we have members join the church who are older than infants who haven't been baptized yet."

"Faith, come on up here to the baptismal." He introduced me and asked the other two families who were baptizing their infants to also join us.

As he sprinkled the infant's heads with water, I bowed my head, knowing my turn was coming. "I baptize you in the name of the Father, the Son, and the Holy Ghost," Pastor Journey blessed us.

I felt the water run down my scalp, and I braced myself for a holy encounter. "Faith Joule, You are a child of God, now part of the body of Christ."

I knew that it represented a new life in Christ. I wasn't turning back; I was running forward to healing. I didn't know what the future held, but I knew who held my future.

I went to sit by Mom and Dad. Grace was sitting behind us. She leaned over and said, "Faith, the water on your head sparkled like diamonds." I smiled and thought, "Maybe there is something special about that water."

CHAPTER 15

SUMMER CAMP

I could hear Mom humming her favorite morning tune as she stretched her vocal cords before she opened my bedroom door. "Time to rise and shine and give God the glory, glory." Mom sang this to me almost every day, but that morning, she hit the high notes with a lot more volume. I put my pillow over my head and groaned. "It's time to go to summer camp, Faith," Mom sang, keeping the melody to the same tune. I was so excited the night before that I could hardly sleep. However, the last couple of hours were so deep that I forgot where I was. I sat up in bed and rubbed my eyes. *Pinch me. Am I dreaming?*

I was already packed, so I ran over to Dezzie's house and tapped on the window. She opened the door with her suitcase in hand. Before we got in the car, Mrs. Diamond and Mom reviewed the checklist, "Did you remember your toothbrush?"

"I'll be right back," I uttered before running back to grab those last-minute items. I saw my journal on my bedside table. I was so glad I went back. I definitely didn't want to forget that. Dezzie's bag had everything she needed and a few more extra items for those of us who may have forgotten.

We rode together to the church, all four of us. Our moms reminded us of all the camp rules along the route, lecturing, "You girls stick together. Be a leader. Help Grace. Keep your bunk clean," Mom reminded us. "And don't forget who you are. You're a Joule and a Diamond– now go, shine your light."

Dezzie and I had been preparing for our first junior high church camp for over a year. Today was the day we'd been waiting for. Hugs and kisses for each mom, and then we finally walked over to the buses. Mrs. Diamond and Mom, along with all the other moms, sat in the parking lot, waving as the bus departed. We pulled out our backpacks to compare snacks. As we opened our gummy bears, Grace got on the bus microphone to make the announcement, "Hello, Summer Campers, we'll stop for a break in 3 hours. Until then, we'll play some games and sing some songs. Does anyone have any requests?"

A hand shot up, "Can we play I Spy?"

After 6 hours and multiple games on a bus, we pulled into the camp parking lot just in time for supper. After we toured our cabin, we claimed our beds in our rooms. Dezzie and I were on the same bunk, the one closest to Grace. We ate burgers in the dining hall, then they shuffled us all out to the beach. The praise team led us in song while we made s'mores around the fire pits that were spread out in the sand. After we hunted for crabs and searched for shooting stars, we went up to the cabin to shower and get ready for bed. We plopped our weary bodies on the beds and talked until Grace led us in a short devotion.

She lectured us about the importance of getting a good night's rest, telling us, "This is just the first night of four nights. You don't want to ruin your week the first night."

Quiet hours started at ten o'clock. She didn't hesitate to turn out the lights. Us girls loved to talk, and if she didn't make us stop, we would stay up all night. After a few jokes and giggles, we all got settled in our bunks. Surprisingly, I fell asleep quickly.

In a deep sleep, I found myself in the Diamond family's backyard. I had not talked to Old Solomon since that fateful night. He didn't know that Bianca passed away, that Grace had become a new friend, or that I started running as a hobby. I wanted to tell him about my baptism and summer camp too. I wanted to tell him how I was using my resources wisely. Running up the stairs, across the bridge, and to the treehouse as fast I could run, I sat down on the floor, gazing up at Old Solomon's gnarled face. I poured out everything that had transpired since our last conversation, realizing that it had been too long.

"Old Solomon, now I understand why you prepared my heart for broken branches. I've not only had a broken arm, but I've also had a broken heart. I've started healing from the inside out. I invited Jesus in my heart, and I've been baptized."

Old Solomon's face came to life, and he yawned.

"Faith, that's good news. Now that you have Jesus, you can talk to Him anytime, anywhere. He is your best source of wisdom."

I nodded in agreement and then responded, "Yes, Old Solomon, I do talk to Jesus, but He doesn't talk back to me. Am I doing something wrong? It's easier to talk to you because I can see you and hear you."

Old Solomon offered his wisdom, "Faith, when you talk to Jesus, do you sit quietly to listen, or do you talk the whole time?"

"I usually talk," I answered.

Old Solomon nodded, and his branches rustled gently in the wind as if in approval. "Faith, when you pray and you worship Jesus, ask Him to speak to you. Then, quiet your mind, remove all distractions, and listen. Would you like to try it here with me?" he suggested.

"Yes, I would Old Solomon. Would you help me, please?" I replied.

Old Solomon continued to guide me, saying, "Faith, hold out your hands with your palms up as if you're going to receive a word from Jesus. Now ask Him to fill you with the Holy Spirit and to open your ears to hear Him. And be quiet. I'll be right here with you."

I did just as Old Solomon instructed. I told Jesus that I was going to be quiet so He could speak. I sat there in the treehouse with Old Solomon, quietly waiting. When a thought would pop into my head, I would try to make it go away as fast as it entered my mind and focus on listening again.

"Old Solomon, I can't keep my mind quiet. Thoughts are flowing in, and I can't make them go away. This is harder than I thought it would be," I complained.

"Faith, imagine you're on a cliff holding a bag. It can be any bag. A garbage bag, a shopping bag, a suitcase. Do you have your bag? Are you standing near the cliff?"

"Yes, Old Solomon, It's my pink and green overnight bag that I take to Dezzie's house. Do I have to stand near the edge?" I inquired, desiring details.

"Yes, Faith, you won't fall. It's only as high as you imagine it. Now open up that bag, and every time you have a thought during your listening time, place that distraction in the bag and throw it over the cliff. Imagine you have many pink and green bags. With each distracting thought, open a bag, put it in, and throw it over the cliff. Go ahead, I'll wait until you're done."

"What if my distracting thought is the treehouse? I can't fit that in my bag, and I certainly can't lift it to throw it over the cliff."

"Faith, this is an imaginary exercise to help you clear your mind. Just shrink it to fit, put it in the bag, and try not to think too hard or too long about it. You aren't hurting anyone or anything. You can go get your thoughts back from the bag after you talk to Jesus. For now, take each thought captive and put those images aside to give Jesus your full attention."

"Yes, sir. I'll try," I conceded.

We both sat quietly while I gathered my thoughts. I put everyone in a bag, including Mom, Dad, and Dezzie. Once I got started, I couldn't stop. Everything that popped in my head went in the bag and over the short cliff. No one had ever given me permission to throw anything or anyone off of a cliff before. This was fun.

"Alright, Old Solomon, where do I go now?" I asked.

Solomon proceeded to instruct me, "Turn around and walk toward the forest. You'll see a narrow river. Walk toward the clear water flowing over the rocks. There's a tree that has fallen in the clearing. Jesus is there. Do you see Him?"

I was amazed at how clearly I could see as I replied, "Yes, I do. He's looking at me too. His arms are wide open, waiting on me."

I ran into Jesus' arms, melting into His side, and cried happy tears. He held my shoulders and looked me in the eye.

I was in awe as Jesus spoke to me, "Faith, I love you, and I have big plans for you, My daughter."

I didn't know what to say, overwhelmed by His love and peaceful presence.

"Faith, do you have anything you want to ask Me?" He inquired.

I hesitated, my heart filled with both curiosity and fear. Finally, I replied, "Yes, Lord, I do, but I don't know how."

Jesus reassured me, saying, "You can trust me. Ask me anything."

With a sense of vulnerability, I responded, "Respectfully Sir, I don't know if I want the answer. If I ask, and I don't like what I hear, I don't know that I can handle it. It was the one distraction that I didn't throw off the cliff. I hold on to it unknowingly. It haunts me. But I'm afraid to ask because I can't take any more disappointments."

Jesus, full of compassion, replied, "Trust Me, Faith. You can ask Me anything."

I took a deep breath, and with the courage that only he could give me, I said, "Everything in my life was good and right, and now it's not. It says in the Bible that we don't have to be afraid. It says that You will always be with us. That You will never leave us nor forsake us. That You will be our shield and protector."

"Yes, Faith, that is all true and a promise that I will always keep. I have always been with you, and I always will be from now until eternity. Go on, Faith, ask Me."

It spilled out as I began to cry, "Where were You the night that my brother's friend got into my bed? Why did you let that happen to me?"

I sobbed harder than I ever had. Unloading that question was like unloading a heavyweight. He waited until I composed myself. Then He said, "Faith, I was there. I cried with you, and I woke your father up to come check on you. I sent Dezzie to give you someone to talk to."

I cried more.

Catching my breath, saying, "But you could have prevented it. You could have."

"Faith, that's what some of the Roman soldiers said when I died on the cross. They said that if I was God, I could have prevented My own death. I didn't allow nor did I prevent sin from entering the world, just as I didn't allow nor prevent My crucifixion and death. The enemy is always stirring up chaos in Christian circles, whether it's homes, churches, or businesses that claim My name. Satan doesn't have to mess with non-Christians. He already has control over them. However, he will pursue Christians, especially new, young Christians, with the intention to lure them to confusion by offering them promises of fame, fortune, and false opportunities. Temporary pleasures only cause you more problems. On the other hand, if you choose righteousness, the easier it will be for you to identify the truth versus the lie. It is important for you to know the truth by reading your Bible and talking to Me. I will warn you, Faith. When you sin, Satan will tempt you to feel shame. You rebuke that shame in My name, telling Satan to flee. Tell him you have been forgiven and are free from shame. This is how it will be until the day I return. Do you understand?"

"Yes, Jesus, I think so. I have another question. When are You coming back to earth?"

"You won't know the day or the time. I won't either. Only God knows."

"Jesus, tell me more about my life. Old Solomon says I have the resources to heal from the inside out. I've accepted You as my Savior and I do believe, Jesus, I do. I know I have a good family, a good church, and good neighbors. Thank You, Jesus, for placing all of these resources in my life to help me. Strangely enough, I want to honor my parents, but I've learned that they can't always protect me. I don't mean to sound ungrateful, but I need safety and security that I don't think they know how to give. I'm protecting myself now, always on the alert, and I'm tired. What can I do to prevent bad things from happening to me? I don't ever want to experience evil ever again. Can I come back to Heaven with You?"

"Faith, you can do anything with Me by your side. My Word will be a lamp to your feet and a light to your path. Read the Bible. Pray. I will guide you."

He opened up His Bible and read 2 Samuel, chapter 13.

Then, he explained, "Tamar, King David's daughter who was raped by her brother, also felt alone," Jesus said.

Surprised to discover that this story was included in the Bible, I inquired, "What happened to her?"

Jesus responded with overflowing compassion, saying, "Faith, I watched over Tamar and the entire household of King David. I never abandoned her, and I won't fail you either. My declaration for both you and Tamar is this: You are holy because I am holy. This is why God sent Me, Faith. I lived and walked on the earth as you do. I endured suffering at the hands of people who abused Me, and I even died for you, Faith. I rose again, and I'm coming back one day. However, until that day arrives, we must work together to build God's kingdom, one saved soul at a time."

"There is hope for me." I nestled into his embrace and said, "Thank You, Jesus."

He continued, "I have many stories like that of Tamar. Remember Jacob's son, Joseph?"

"Yes, I love the story of Joseph and his coat of many colors."

"Did his life end because he was rejected by his brothers?" Jesus asked.

"No, it didn't," I answered.

"That's right. Joseph was separated from the earthly father who loved him, but he recognized that I was his Heavenly Father. He knew Me, and he chose to serve Me well. He understood his own history and claimed My promises for his life. You and I will fight some battles, and we will win, together. Like Joseph, who grew wiser and stronger throughout his hardships, suffering will make you stronger."

"Yes, You're the second person who has told me that. Well, Old Solomon is a tree, and he told me that in my dream," I recalled.

Jesus continued, "Remember, the story ends with Joseph, in obedience, forgiving his brothers, and, as a result, he was blessed above and beyond measure. He understood what his brothers meant for evil, I used for good. It is the same for you, Faith. Seek opportunities to use your suffering for good, and be kind to those who hurt you when they show true repentance."

"Yes, Sir. Thank You, Jesus. I'm learning so many new and wonderful things. I feel like a weight has been lifted. When can I talk to You again?"

"Faith, that is totally up to you. I never sleep, so feel free to talk to Me anytime."

All of a sudden, a flash of light shone in my face. I was awakened by Grace, "Rise and Shine, it's BBB time. That translates to breakfast, Bible study, and beach time. Grab your Bibles, journals, a pen, and meet me in the sand in 10 minutes."

Where am I? Then, it all came back to me. I was at summer camp. I glanced around the room at the other bunk beds filled with sleepy girls stirring as they woke up. Dezzie was in the bunk above me.

Whispering in a groggy voice, I yawned and said, "Dezzie, I just had the most vivid dream. I was talking to Jesus. It was so real."

We walked down to the sandy shore in our pajamas, forming a circle as we settled on our towels. Grace gave us a warm welcome, offering us donuts and juice. She reviewed the schedule for the first day at camp. Then she said, "Before we begin our Bible study, I have a special assignment for you. The beach is the perfect setting for a conversation with Jesus. Spread out, and silently pray, praise, or worship quietly. This is your time with Jesus. Ask Him to open your heart and mind to what He wants to teach you this week. I encourage you to journal your prayers. You may find it rewarding to look back at the end of the week and see how your prayers have been answered. I'll call you all back together in fifteen minutes."

I walked up to the water's edge, facing the ocean stretched out in front of me. I placed my towel in the sand and sat down. I opened my journal and began to write. My pen struggled to keep pace with the incoming waves of thoughts and memories from my dream. When I had recorded as much as I could recall, I closed my eyes and offered a prayer.

"Dear Jesus, if our conversation last night was real, and the words you spoke to me were genuine, please show me now."

I recalled the guided prayer that Old Solomon taught me. I walked to the short cliff, opened my bag, and threw in everything that was distracting me. I imagined myself walking to the forest, and there He was with open arms, waiting for me. I sat down on the log beside Him.

In my spirit, I heard a whisper, "Open your eyes. Look up, My child."

I looked at the ocean with the waves crashing in, the morning sun reflecting off of the top of the water as the ripples moved in constant motion.

"Yes, it was Me, Faith," He affirmed. "Just as the ocean stretches out before you now, so am I. I was with you, and I always will be. In this world, you will face challenges, but I have overcome the world. I will never abandon you. Do not be afraid. I am by your side always. When doubt creeps in, think of the ocean and be assured that I am deeper and wider than anything the world offers you. Take that leap, Faith. I've got you."

Then I heard Grace behind us announcing, "It's time to gather around for Bible study. Come on back to the circle."

I stood up, held my hands high, and praised Him, "Thank you, Jesus."

As I walked back to our group, Grace looked at me and said, "Faith, you are glowing. Would you like to tell us about your quiet time?"

"Of course, I'd love to share. Last night, I had an extraordinary dream, where I was in conversation with Jesus. I often have vivid dreams. Last night, it was both the tree and Jesus, making it the most realistic dream I've ever experienced. So, this morning, I journaled everything that Jesus and I discussed. Then, I asked Him to confirm whether our conversation was indeed real. After clearing my mind of all distractions, I felt His presence all around me, confirming those very words. I am so grateful for the quiet time you provided us this morning. I needed to know that Jesus is who He said He is and that His words were truly spoken to me. Thank you."

Grace started our morning study, saying, "That is a good segue into our Bible study today. Do you girls believe that Jesus can speak to you?"

I was the only one that raised my hand.

Grace asked me again to share.

"Faith, do you mind sharing how you came to hear Jesus?"

"Grace, if you would have asked me the same question yesterday, my answer would have been entirely different. But I had a friend who guided me. He said that now that I have Jesus in my heart, that I can hear directly from Him."

I walked the girls through removing the distractions at the cliff, using the bag, and walking to the forest, the babbling brook, and the log.

Grace said, "Girls, that is a beautiful way to approach prayer. Listening to God does require a quiet place without distractions.

If you are prone to leading conversations with Jesus, you'll want to practice being quiet and letting Him lead. If that makes you uncomfortable, just pray about it. Ask Jesus to help you calm your heart. He is always with you, so reach out and talk to Him. The more you pray and read your Bible, the more you will know who Jesus is and the closer you will be to Him. Knowing Him will allow you to be more comfortable sharing about Him. And that leads me to the theme of our week."

She explained, "You may have noticed all of the potted plants and flowers in the large auditorium. The theme for the week was 'Planting Seeds.' At the end of the week, you will take a plant or flower home to remind you of everything you learned, and hopefully, as you water your plant and care for it, you'll remember to share Jesus with a friend."

On the walk back up to the bunkhouse, Dezzie asked me, "Faith, I want to know more about talking to Jesus. I have some questions for Him."

"Let's ask Grace if we can stay in the bunkhouse during the morning games, and we'll pray instead."

Grace thought that was a good idea. "Sure girls, I'll come back and get you in one hour."

I pulled out my journal and read to her everything that Jesus told me last night in my dreams and again this morning.

"It's proof that He really does love us and knows everything. Let me walk you through the process like Old Solomon walked me through it. Then, you will know too. Don't be afraid to ask Him the hard questions. He can handle it. I promise," I said.

She wanted to believe me but expressed her doubts, saying, "But Faith, why did bad things happen to us? We gave Him our hearts, and we were baptized. We have been helping our neighbors. We have been good. We haven't done anything wrong. I just don't understand."

"Dezzie, let me walk you through the prayer, and you tell Jesus everything you told me and ask Him. He will tell you the truth."

I walked Dezzie through freeing her mind from distractions and, then through the forest to Jesus. Then, I was quiet as she prayed and talked to Jesus. After some time went by, Grace quietly walked back into the room. Dezzie was crying. She mouthed, "I'll be back later."

Dezzie finally looked up. "I got a word from Jesus. He told me about Lazarus, and He read to me from John, Chapter 11. He said He saw how saddened I was about Bianca's death. He said He was in the hospital room with her and laid His body over hers to give her eternal life in Heaven. He also told me about our bodies. Faith, our bodies are part of the church, a stone of the temple to Him. We are to care for our body, minds, hearts, and do our part, as we help care for others."

I looked at Dezzie and confirmed, "Jesus spoke truth to us regarding our specific situations. We have no reason to doubt that we are truly His and that we are going to help girls like us in the future. We have to stay strong." I gave her a big hug. She was the happiest she had been in a long time.

"Speaking of taking care of our bodies, I'm hungry. Let's eat."

We walked over to the conference center just in time for lunch.

CHAPTER 16

THE LAST NIGHT AT SUMMER CAMP

Later that week:

On the last night of camp, they transported us by bus out to a local farm. Under a large white tent, the pastor, dressed in his blue jean overalls and trucker cap, stood beside a large tractor.

"Welcome to the farm. We've been talking about Mark, chapter 4, all week, so I thought this little trip to the farm might help you remember it. I brought the seeds, tools, water, and a Bible. All you'll have to do is open your ears and your hearts. Let me set the scene for you. Imagine this pasture out here as your heart. Some of you have good soil, but some of you need to pull some weeds, till the ground, and add fertilizer to help the truths of God's Word settle and take root in your heart. Like these crops, or even a small home garden, there's always work to be done. What does a farmer do to keep his crops free from predators and disease? We're going to talk about some of those things tonight.

"As I look out over the crowd, I see potential. You all have the possibility of becoming a garden who produces good fruit. However, some of you are completely distracted by the ambiance, wondering why in the world we left the beach for a farm. When Jesus told the story of a farmer in Mark, He was near the water. I bet the disciples, like you, were a little confused as to why Jesus chose the story of sowing seed. After all, He used his boat as a pulpit instead of a tractor. On the other hand, some of you are completely locked in with anticipation of the next few minutes. Imagine Jesus in the water, on a boat, saying these words."

He prayed, saying, "Dear Jesus, open the eyes, ears, and hearts of these students today so they can see You, hear You, and love You. Amen." He read Mark 4 again. "Who is the farmer in this story? Some say Jesus, some say pastors. I say both. I'll even dare to say it might be you. Are you willing to share God's message?"

The white canvas sack on the pastor's shoulder was heavy with seed. He reached in and threw some seed in front of him. Holding a tiny seed in his hand held high, he emphasized the importance of nurturing our own soil.

"This seed cannot take root if the soil is not prepared. For us, our hearts and minds are the soil." He grabbed a shovel and asked, "What weeds need to be dug out of your heart tonight? What sin have you allowed to take root that needs to be extracted? Are you struggling with jealousy, anger, discontentment? Perhaps you're caught in a web of lies, or you have hate in your heart for someone. Have you hurt someone and need to reconcile? Do you need to forgive those who have hurt you? Do you believe God can help you remove all of the weeds that keep good fruit from growing in your heart? These are questions that you'll need to tend to. Do not ignore the weeds, or they will choke out your faith."

This message instantly evoked memories of my encounter with Old Solomon when he told me about bitter roots that cause disease and death in a tree. The pastor continued with his message, saying, "Once the soil of our heart is prepared, we can sow the seeds, we can water them, but it's only by the 'Son light' of God that true flourishing occurs. Your part in the Christian walk is surrender and obedience. Give Him your heart and watch what He can do."

What a relief for me. Personally, the thought of shouldering the weight of mine or someone else's salvation might have led me to give up before even starting. Given my past experiences, on my own, I will make mistakes. But realizing that I can play a role in planting seeds or watering someone's faith without the pressure of making them grow allows me to share Jesus without fear of failure. I can't mess salvation up. I'm not that important. Jesus has my back.

He warned us, saying, "Beware of bad weather. The most important part of farming is weather. The perfect balance of good soil, rain, and sun is paramount in raising crops. If there is no rain or water or no sun, the seed won't sprout or ever produce food to eat. So it is with life. We need to shower ourselves in prayer, read the Word of God, and know the Son of God in order for our spiritual life to grow. When the storms come and the wind blows in, will you be strong enough to stand?" He paused and scanned the crowd, locking eyes with some as if he knew them personally.

"Some of you know what storms of life I'm talking about. You've experienced trouble at home or at school. You've seen divorce and death."

I looked at Dezzie and didn't have to say a word. She and I know the kind of storms he was preaching about.

He challenged us to pray silently about the garden of our hearts, imagining our soul as a garden to be cared for as a farmer tends to his land. His ultimate challenge was to find an accountability partner. He said, "Unlike this pasture where you can see the results of hard work, our spiritual state isn't seen by the naked eye. We can easily hide sin that grows in our hearts. Or can we? With a close friend who is willing to tell you the hard truths and accept your words of encouragement, your fruit will grow even better.

"As a farmer sharpens his blades for the harvest, so we must sharpen one another." He ended in a prayer for us. I'm so thankful that Dezzie and I had the opportunity to come to camp together. She and I committed to keeping an account of one another's 'garden' and sharpening one another.

After the sermon, they had a full farm experience waiting on us. We rode horses, fed the animals, and even enjoyed a long hayride around the trail in and out of the forest of the farm. At dark, we rode the bus back to the beach, singing portions of a few of our favorite country music songs about farms and tractors before we arrived back at the retreat center.

"You girls meet me out at the beach in fifteen minutes," Grace announced.

To our surprise, there was a large white cross that stood near our group's circle of chairs that was not there before. A large spotlight shone on it as if to say, "If you haven't learned anything all week, Jesus is the reason we're here."

Along the beach, fires burned in large metal pots for the small groups to circle around to meet. Each chair had a blanket, a plate of chocolates, marshmallows, graham crackers, and roasting sticks. The setting could not have been more inviting.

Under the star-studded sky, Grace gathered us around our fire for one more small group meeting, saying, "I have enjoyed this week with each of you. When I dedicated my life to helping girls like you to know Jesus, I had no idea I would have this much fun. It's good to enjoy camp, but I want more for you. I want you to leave here with good soil." Spurring on conversations about the week, she asked us, "What was your favorite part of camp and why?"

One by one, each girl spoke up, answering her question. Most everyone expressed their enjoyment of the music and the beach. Dezzie answered at length, saying, "I've had such a good time. I never knew a church camp could be this much fun. I really like the theme of sowing seeds, also. After all, science is my favorite subject."

I answered next, saying, "The first day was my favorite day. I especially enjoyed the mornings, walking out to the beach at sunrise for Bible time. Grace, do you mind if I walk over to the cross? I would like to take something that I've been holding on to. I need to lay it down at the foot of the cross and give it to Jesus fully."

Grace answered, "Sure, Faith, we'll all go over there as a group in a little bit. Do you mind me asking you what you might need to lay down? If it's private, and you prefer not to share aloud with the group, there is no pressure to share."

I answered her, "That first morning when I told you about the prayer process that I've been using, the first step is to put all of our distractions in a bag. I have one distraction that I can't put in the bag and throw over the cliff. No matter how hard I try, I don't know how to let it go. Maybe if I lay it down tonight, here, instead of in my mind, it will help me. I need to lay it at the cross and stop trying to carry it around all on my own. I have it written down on this paper."

Grace had a better idea, saying, "Faith, I want you to not only lay that distraction down at Christ's feet, but I also want you to allow Jesus to refine you through the healing process. Did you know that fire is used in the refining process to purify elements like sugar and precious metals? When we let the fire of Christ refine us,

He removes impurities. Jesus is like our fire, refining us. Faith, I could be wrong, but if you lay that paper at the foot of that cross, it may get blown away. What if you were to throw it in the fire pit, praying that Jesus knows your heart. He will refine you."

I nodded my head and said, "Yes, I like that better."

She looked up at all of the girls and encouraged them, saying, "If anyone else has something they would like to write down, I have extra paper and pens here. We can all write down our worries, our fears, those cares that never seem to go away, and we can give them to Jesus tonight, thrown in the fire, believing that He will save us."

That was just what we all needed to hear. Everyone wrote down their concerns and prayers. One by one, we quietly approached the fire pit and dropped in our papers.

One girl asked, "If I write down my worries and concerns, and I pray for them, but I haven't given my heart to Jesus, will He answer my prayers?"

"That's a good question." Grace explained, "In the Bible when we read about Jesus healing the blind and the mute, the crippled, and the demon-possessed, Jesus says, 'It's your faith that has healed you.' We don't know if those who were healed from their earthly handicap were truly saved from death and given eternal life like we are today. However, I do know that Jesus isn't Santa. We don't use Him to get what we want at the moment. We worship Him for who He is, God's Son, and what He's done, died on the cross, and rose again for you and me. In John 3:16, when Jesus talked to Nicademous, the Jewish priest, He told him that in order to be in Heaven eternally, that being born again was necessary. If you haven't asked Jesus to be your Savior, then do it tonight. This doesn't have to be a sad ending to a great week. This can be an amazing beginning to righteous life. He will answer you."

Grace offered to pray with the girls who wanted to ask Jesus in their hearts. Right then and there, the girls who were not believers in Jesus raised their hand, and repeating after Grace, asked Jesus to be the Savior. I looked at Dezzie, leaned over, and drew a cross, a triangle, and a heart in the sand. She looked at me, smiling, and said, "Jesus changes hearts."

What an unforgettable night it was. The water surged like Jesus in the hearts of these girls. We spent the entire night gathered around a blazing fire. Amidst our tears and our laughter, our shared sisterhood in Christ became abundantly clear through the overwhelming joy that enveloped us all.

CHAPTER 17

BRIGHT LIGHT WORSHIP NIGHTS

One Week Later

Dezzie and I lugged our blankets and pillows up the staircase leading to the Bright Light Treehouse, anticipating another Friday night sleepover. The summer evening unfolded with another bright idea as the moon's glow bathed us with radiant light through the window. It provided just enough illumination for us to immerse ourselves in a tranquil night of reading and journaling.

"What an incredibly crazy busy week it's been. I'm truly grateful it's finally Friday," I said as I plopped my tired body on the blanket.

Our "Daddy's Angels" duties were growing, and we were weary from the responsibilities of the week. We'd cared for little Paul, launched a reading and craft club hour at the neighborhood clubhouse, and even pulled weeds out of Mr. O'Conner's overgrown flower beds. In addition, we were now proud owners of our new puppies, Michie and Gabby, named after the angels of the Bible, Michael and Gabriel. Our moms were right; they do require a lot of attention.

Opening a bag of freshly popped popcorn, I mused, "Can you believe it's been a whole week since we left camp?"

Dezzie responded, her eyes reflecting the shimmer of a new-found perspective, "Summer camp feels like a glimpse of Heaven."

"I've been thinking about the timing of the recent months—the construction of the treehouse, starting Daddy's Angels, our decision to follow Jesus, and the hard times we faced. I wouldn't wish hard times on anyone, but I pray more each day for God's protection. And I feel His love is so close to me that I talk to Him a lot more now. That's something I never did before."

Dezzie agreed with me, saying, "Everything at camp, from the worship, singing, and fellowship, was so encouraging. Wouldn't it be nice if every day was like camp? You know what I mean? I wish I didn't have to wait until next summer."

Dezzie's words sparked an idea within me, "That's a fantastic idea, Dezzie." I said. "While we can't have church camp every day, why not create something special once a week? We can pattern it after camp with worship, prayer, and fellowship together. Your backyard would be the perfect place, and the treehouse could serve as the podium for whoever wishes to share."

Thinking out loud, Dezzie said, "Grace could lead us on Sunday nights like she did at camp. We could invite other youth groups to join us."

"That's a good start," I added.

We spent the majority of the night crafting our plans for the inaugural praise and worship night, knowing that it was destined to be a brilliant event.

The following morning, Dezzie and I shared our idea with our moms.

Dezzie talked to her Mom in a compassionate way, saying, "Mom, I know that our family has been so sad lately. Faith and I have an idea. We want kids who didn't go to camp to experience a camp-like atmosphere each week here at our house. We think opening our home and our backyard for kids like us will help them to know that there is something greater than ourselves. We want them to find hope. And we have the perfect space."

Mrs. Diamond wasted no time, saying, "I really like this idea," and promptly sent out a message to the neighborhood and local churches via email: "Calling all sixth and seventh grade children! Praise and Worship Night at the Diamonds' House, next Sunday night, July 7th at 6pm."

Every evening after work, we helped our parents work to transform the backyard into a warm and inviting space, adding even more decorations and lights.

Sunday, July 7th at 6pm.

On the Sunday of the inaugural Bright Light Praise and Worship Night, at six o'clock, a crowd gathered around. Grace took a step forward and addressed the gathering, "We want to express our gratitude to all of you for joining us in the first backyard lighting ceremony. Dezzie and Faith wish for everyone to see these lights and understand that Jesus is the Light, and within Him, we find the light of life."

With eager anticipation, we began a countdown, "three, two, one." We plugged in the lights. Suddenly, the whole backyard burst into brilliance, brighter than it had ever been before. It resembled a Christmas scene in the middle of July, with lights adorning every tree, including Old Solomon, and even the treehouse. Once again, our dads had worked hard to make our dreams a reality.

Grace ascended to the balcony of the treehouse and addressed the gathering, saying, "A warm welcome to each and every one of you at the Bright Light Worship Night. I want to extend our heartfelt gratitude to Faith, Dezzie, and their families for hosting this event. May this evening mark the start of numerous occasions for us to come together for fellowship. May we discover how to carry our light from this place to our neighbors and communities."

"I'd like to invite Faith and Dezzie to come on up to the balcony," Grace announced, introducing us to the crowd who gathered in the Diamond's backyard. "I had the privilege of meeting these girls at church. These young ladies share a desire to see each one of you here to grow in your faith in Jesus. They understand firsthand that life can be filled with challenges and difficulties, and that, we all encounter dark moments along the way. But even in those moments, we have a light to shine."

Dezzie and I distributed flashlights to everyone, a special gift for the occasion. Each flashlight came adorned with a sticker displaying John 1:5, "The light shines in the darkness, and the darkness has not overcome it."

Mr. Diamond chimed in, "I'm going to strum 'This Little Light of Mine' on the guitar. Feel free to turn on your flashlights and join in singing along with me if you know the song."

As the lights illuminated, the collective worship, the vibrant group of kids, and the music enveloped me, bringing back memories of camp. At that moment, I sensed that this was the life I wanted to embrace every single day.

Grace lifted her flashlight, using it to illustrate her point about Jesus as the light.

"Light is a recurring theme throughout the Bible, from its inception when God created light in Genesis, to the conclusion. The last book of the Bible is Revelation. The twenty-second chapter, verse 5, says, 'And the night will be no more. They will need no light of lamp or sun, for the Lord God will be their light, and they will reign forever and ever,'" Grace explained. "Have you ever considered the ongoing battle between the light and the darkness? Just look around at all the lights in the trees and the flashlights. Which one emerges victorious? Light or darkness?"

In unison, everyone responded, "Light."

"That's right. Now, I want you all to turn off your flashlights."

Dezzie and I disconnected the lights, and all of the flashlights were extinguished. The darkness that surrounded us was profound. Grace continued, "The darkness is very deep. Without Jesus in our hearts, our hearts are very dark. We must invite Jesus to bring His light, because we can't generate that light on our own. He is the source."

Grace illuminated her flashlight, demonstrating a powerful point. "Do you see how my small light alone can dispel so much darkness? When one sinner embraces belief, the sin begins to retreat. Now, I invite each of you to turn your flashlights back on."

The crowd responded by flicking on their flashlights, creating a collective glow that spread and illuminated the surroundings. Then she instructed us, "Girls, go ahead and plug in the tree lights." Dezzie and I promptly plugged the stringed lights, filling the area with even more radiance.

With enthusiasm, Grace shared, "Now, together, we have completely conquered the darkness."

Before she could say anything more, the crowd erupted with applause.

After that night, the children invited more children. The crowd grew each week. Parents attended out of curiosity, wondering what all the excitement was about. The week before school started, we had our largest attendance yet. Grace delivered a message centered on the Lord's Prayer.

She began, "One of the wonderful benefits of our relationship with Jesus is the privilege of communicating with Him through prayer. In various churches, we recite the Lord's Prayer, or as some refer to it, the Our Father Prayer."

Grace then turned to the New Testament, quoting the passage where Jesus instructed His disciples in the art of prayer. She continued, "Many of us have recited this prayer in church and even at our sporting events. But do we merely say these words, or do we really mean them? Have you ever taken a moment to deeply contemplate the meaning behind each word? Tonight, I would like to consider the seven key elements in this prayer."

She elaborated, "First, when we say, 'Our Father who is in Heaven, hallowed is Your name,' we are addressing God as holy or greatly honored. It's a phrase of utmost respect. We'll conclude our evening with this prayer, and I encourage each of you to recite it with reverence, internalizing each and every word."

As Grace delved into the elements of the Lord's Prayer, my inner thoughts echoed, "Yes, thank You, Jesus."

Grace proceeded, "Secondly, we engage in worship and praise, acknowledging who God is and all the magnificent deeds He has accomplished."

And I responded with heartfelt gratitude, "Yes, thank You for your boundless goodness."

Grace then moved on to the third element of the Lord's prayer, explaining, "We recognize that God's will and plans are perfect, acknowledging His control. We acknowledge our imperfection and surrender control to Him, trusting that He knows what's best for us."

Though I hesitated momentarily, I acknowledged the truth in her teachings, saying, "Yes, Lord, let Your will be done, even when I don't fully comprehend it."

Grace continued, "Next, we humbly present our wants and needs before God. Notice that this is the fourth part of the prayer, not the first. We don't just rush into prayer with our desires."

Her words captured my attention, prompting me to contemplate the significance of the sequence. Shifting her focus from the supplication to forgiveness, she said, "The following part of the Lord's prayer is deeply personal. 'And forgive us our sins as we forgive those who sin against us.'"

She paused to clarify an important point, dwelling for a moment on the variations in phrasing, where some say "debts" or "trespasses" instead of "sins." She explained that "debts" refer to something owed, signifying that one has taken or borrowed something that does not belong to them, while "trespassing" involves entering someone's property without permission or committing an offense against another.

Her tone grew markedly serious when she declared, "If we fail to forgive others for their sins, debts, or trespasses against us, then we will not receive forgiveness when we, in turn, sin, owe, or trespass against someone else. Forgiving others isn't a mere choice, it's a command. Forgiveness, although at times emotionally challenging, is an essential component for a life in Christ. We are commanded to extend forgiveness to others, just as He forgave us. The very purpose of Christ's life, death, and resurrection revolves around forgiveness. We mustn't omit this part of the prayer. It may well be the most vital part."

At that moment, I found myself at a crossroads in my faith, feeling a profound sense of fear. Doubt began to creep in as I questioned whether I truly could forgive, and, if I couldn't, then I knew that I would be abandoning my faith.

Grace was still speaking. She concluded with two final elements of the Lord's Prayer. She emphasized that we seek protection and guidance in overcoming sin and the attacks of Satan, giving God the glory for His boundless power.

Grace acknowledged the weight of her message, saying, "I realize that I have given you all much to ponder. I have printed an explanation of the Lord's Prayer for you to take home and reflect upon. If anyone has any questions or seeks further discussion, I'll be in the treehouse after our prayer. You can join me there."

As soon as Grace uttered, "Amen," I ran to the steps and clambered up to the treehouse as quickly as I could get there. Words tumbled out of me before I even had a chance to open the door to the treehouse. "Grace, we need to talk," I began urgently. "I can't do this."

"Can't do what, Faith?" Grace asked.

"I can't bring myself to forgive someone else's offense against me. It's impossible for me to take that step," I lamented.

"Slow down, Faith. Tell me what you're thinking," Grace said.

"I feel like there's nothing left of me to give." I had to take a breath, then I kept unloading my thoughts. "I'm tirelessly striving to regain something that can never be restored. I'm trying to be a good Christian, to be nice, to regain peace in my life, have compassion for others, and to remain humble. But, when it comes to forgiveness, I simply can't."

"Faith, I'm listening, and I want you to know that I've walked in your shoes. I completely empathize with your pain and sorrow." Grace responded gently. "However, we can't selectively choose the parts of the Christian life or the Lord's Prayer we like and disregard the rest. The truth is still the truth. It is essential that we answer the call to forgive."

"How? Tell me how."

"This is a spiritual battle you're facing, and you have been subjected to an attack. Your battle isn't against a person, Faith, your battle is against spiritual forces that have waged a war for your soul. You can win this war with Jesus by your side. You have to decide if you'll fight or will you retreat?"

"This is not fair!" I grumbled to myself..

She continued, her voice filled with compassion, "You stand at a monumental crossroads, Faith. It's a choice that will shape your spiritual journey. Either you commit one hundred percent to Christ, or you choose to give Him zero percent. There's no middle ground in the Christian life. You can either live as a victim, forever trapped and unable to grow spiritually, or you can emerge as a survivor in Christ, living a life of victory. The choice is yours."

In tears, I cried out, "That's not fair! How could He expect me to forgive someone who took something so deeply personal from me? I didn't do anything wrong."

"Faith, holding on to unforgiveness doesn't benefit you in any way. In truth, it only causes you harm. Over time, anger festers into bitterness and malice, slowly eating away at you from the inside out. It's a gradual decline that weakens your spirit," Grace emphasized.

I glanced over at Old Solomon, "Did he tell you to say that?"

Grace raised an eyebrow and looked up.

Just then, Dezzie knocked on the door and entered, her concern evident. "Can I come in? Everyone has left. It's just us now," she said, noting my tear-stained red face. Turning to me, she asked, "Faith, what's wrong?"

"Dezzie, I won't forgive him. You'll have to continue on with this Christian journey without me," I declared with a heavy heart.

But Dezzie, refusing to accept my announcement, responded, "No, Faith, I won't let you give up. We're in this fight together. Right here, right now, let's make another promise to each other to face forgiveness head-on. We are Daddy's Angels, and we don't shy away from challenges."

Grace interjected, "Your journey so far has been marked by fearlessness, supported by a supernatural heavenly strength. Both of you girls are under the protection of a force much mightier than any coward. Remember, Satan is the ultimate loser. Don't be deceived into believing that you have earned that anger. Let it go, and let Jesus help you. He conquers this battle, and we triumph alongside Him."

I was taken aback by the authority and conviction in Dezzie and Grace's words, realizing that they both spoke with a depth of understanding and determination that I had never witnessed before.

CHAPTER 18

FORGIVEN

The next week at the Bright Light Praise and Worship night, Grace shared her testimony of forgiveness.

Grace asked us to raise our hands if we've ever had to forgive. Everyone's hand went up. "Yes, we all have forgiven offenses."

She turned her talk to us in the crowd with a request, saying, "Imagine someone in your mind who you have yet to forgive. Keep that person's image in your thoughts for the next few minutes."

She's so good at helping us stay focused on the topic. "Unforgiveness," she imparted, "Is a heavy burden that many of us carry. Someone has offended us, caused us harm, or hurt us in some way. Instead of kindly confronting the person to reconcile the situation quickly, we often retreat, offering excuses that only prolong the healing of our hearts."

Then, she asked a more thought-provoking question, saying, "You don't have to raise your hand or voice your opinion, but I want you to consider this. Is there a sin that you deem unforgivable?"

There was a brief pause, giving us a moment to reflect. Then she asked us, "Would Jesus forgive that sin?"

She went on to explain, "The unforgivable sin is forgivable. Jesus forgives every sinner who turns from their sins and believes in him, even murderers and thieves." She continued, saying, "And, in time, you can too."

Grace proceeded to recount the story of Joseph from the book of Genesis. She detailed how Joseph's brothers, fueled by jealousy, had cast him into a pit, only to be discovered by passing travelers who sold him into slavery in Egypt. Many years later, during a famine, their father, Jacob, sent them to Egypt, where Joseph had risen to a position of power. His brothers begged for their own survival.

She spoke with compassion, saying, "Despite the cruelty Joseph had endured at the hands of his brothers, God had greatly blessed him. Joseph was no longer a slave, but through his hard work, perseverance, and obedience to the call of God in his life, Joseph had been elevated to a position of authority alongside Pharaoh. He had the power to bless his brothers, even though he wasn't obligated to do so. He could have turned them away or sought revenge, leaving them to suffer." She interrupted the story and asked, "What would the world advise us to do in such a situation?"

Continuing with the story that she knew so well, she said, "Joseph's brothers failed to recognize him, and it would have been easy for him to disregard them. However, he chose a different path by extending an invitation to them, providing food, and ensuring the well-being of both them and their families. Joseph, guided by his faith in God, made the righteous choice. He forgave them and reassured them with these words, 'Don't be afraid. Am I in the place of God? You meant to harm me, but God meant it for good to bring about the present result–the survival of many people. So, do not be afraid. I will provide for you and your little ones.' The account continued saying that he reassured them and spoke kindly to them. Joseph knew that the punishment of sins belongs to God, not to mankind.

"Thanks to Joseph's obedience, his family not only survived but also played a vital role in the lineage leading to the birth of Jesus. Even thousands of years after their time on earth, we continue to draw valuable lessons from Joseph and Jesus. In the same way, your act of forgiveness can act as a powerful testimony, demonstrating God's grace for others."

She encouraged us, knowing that difficult days were ahead of us, "If you find forgiveness challenging, remember that you don't have to go through it alone. Reach out for support from a friend if you need it."

She was nearly finished with her talk, but there was one more crucial point she wanted to emphasize. She stated, "The pinnacle of both Jesus's story and our own life story is forgiveness. You have been saved today because you accepted His forgiveness. Now, go and follow Him. Be completely free and allow yourself to forgive."

Following her message, Grace made herself available at the front for anyone seeking counsel or prayer. Her message had such a profound impact that, by the end of the night, fifteen people came forward, seeking prayer and guidance to find forgiveness for those who had hurt them.

We realized that we were not alone in our experiences. We felt a calling to address the needs of these children who came forward, recognizing that forgiveness is a journey.

That week, we reached out to each of them individually and invited them to join us for a small group study an hour before our Praise and Worship session. To our delight, they all agreed to participate. It marked Grace's inaugural Small Group Session. This gathering not only provided support to Dezzie and me but also introduced us to friends who could relate to our experiences, offering each other a glimmer of hope.

Our newfound mission was clear: to assist children in their journey toward healing from those who have hurt them. Witnessing the number of young people who came forward in our small community, we couldn't help but imagine the countless others who might be in need, including those who didn't attend church or youth meetings. There was, sadly, an unmistakable and pressing need in our community that we could not afford to ignore.

As these new relationships grew and more heartache was revealed, the path to our future was paved. We dedicated ourselves to a future of aiding children trapped in hurtful situations. The needs were so great that our own personal budgets could not support them. We found resources in our community to assist many of these children, but there was a lack for others. Quitting was not a choice. A lack of funds was only a stepping stone to our next idea.

Grace shared, "When I was in seminary, we volunteered our time at shelters for the homeless, for the abused, and for the needy. There are so many hurting people, especially children. You could be specific in your fundraising. Who do you want to serve and why?" Grace asked.

"I see a need for children, like Joseph, but specifically, for girls. How about a shelter for girls seeking safe haven who are running from abusive homes?" I offered.

Grace agreed, "I can attest to the fact that the need is real."

Our parents exchanged glances, their expressions revealing their surprise at the scale of our vision. "We can't accomplish anything alone. We need your support," Dezzie insisted. "Mom, can you send out another email to the churches letting them know about our idea? We're going to need their prayers and support as well as donations."

Word quickly spread, and donations started pouring in. In the meantime, as we researched "temporary safe space for children," we didn't find anywhere that offered that narrow of a focus. We didn't have anywhere to send our money. So, we realized our next Daddy's Angel's mission, and the idea for the Bright Light Safe House shelter was born.

CHAPTER 19

RETURNING TO HOPE

"That's my story, and that's how I got here. It's hard to believe it was ten years ago," I said, looking around Grace's office, "Here we are now, Hope, sitting in an office in that very shelter. What once was a dream and a prayer is now a reality."

Hope was on the edge of her seat, taking in my every word. I wondered if my story resonated with her when she asked, "How much money does it take to buy and renovate a place like this?"

How did my story of healing cause her to think about money? I thought. Maybe I wasn't clear that the money was a miracle, but most importantly, Jesus changing my heart is the biggest miracle of all. So I tried to explain, saying, "One night, out of the blue, Daddy received a text from a friend who was a realtor that read, 'Take a look at this church on the auction site. Starting bid is fifty thousand. The crime in that area has brought the real estate prices down to a minimum. We need to bring some light back into that community. Any ideas?'

"Dad showed us the text, saying, "This is precisely why we must continue to spread the love of Jesus. Even churches are shutting down. I think this is our opportunity, girls."

"We prayed at that very moment that if God wanted us to have that church, that He would open the doors and allow us in. We had enough money from tithes and donations in our Bright Light Worship Night Fund. Dad called his friend and asked him to place the bid. The next morning, we all loaded up to go visit this old church downtown. His friend met us there. We gave him a check, and he gave us the keys. We were new owners of an old, run-down church that had been ignored and vandalized, but we were ecstatic. It was that easy. It was a sure sign that God approved the offer.

"After a year of meeting with an architect, drafting and planning a safe house, we started the demolition. It's taken us all these years to complete the renovation, and now, we're adding on.

Thanks to the generous donors, we've been able to keep this place thriving. The response from the community has been truly remarkable. Not only have parents contributed generous sums, but an anonymous donor gave a substantial amount, more than enough to enable our fathers to completely renovate this very church. God's presence is evident, and his blessings are abundant in this place.

"Many loving people have given time and attention to this building, including the fifteen children who came forward that night for prayerful support. Not only were they part of our first small group, but they all have contributed to the original structure. Whether writing Bible verses on the newly-poured floors and beams, carrying in boxes of tile, to painting the walls, the hands that have touched this place have prayed for you and this very moment.

"I truly believe that everything happens for a reason. You are here because it is God's will for you to heal and be a blessing. Hope, this is only temporary discomfort. There is a bigger picture. God can use your past and turn it around for good if you let Him. I pray you can see beyond today. There's purpose in the pain. It's not for the here and now. It's for the eternal glory of God. Believe it. Have faith that Jesus will use your suffering for His glory."

Still fixated on the money we raised and the time that it took to establish the safe house, Hope commented, "That's a lot of hard work and money raised over many years for some girls who have been abused." She tilted her head and asked, "You sacrificed all that for girls like me?" Looking down at her feet, mumbling, "We're not worth all of that."

"You are worth so much more than that, Hope. In Romans 5:8, Paul says you are worth so much that Jesus laid his life down for you. The creator God, King of kings and Lord of lords, sent His Son, Jesus, down from a perfect Heaven to a sinful world to be born, to live, and to die a painful, agonizing death on the cross for you. He loves you, Hope. Your life is precious. You're worth a whole lot more than this building. What we have built here is only a tiny fraction of what God can do when we give Him our life. In God's economy, Christ is life, and His riches are a mystery. He takes us as we are, delivers us from this natural sin-stained flesh, redeems us, and makes us sinless. No price tag can be placed on a saved, transformed, spiritual life. We work for God, who can turn five fish and two loaves into a feast that feeds thousands. Heaven's economy doesn't include dollars."

Oliver came to the door and said, "Excuse me ladies, but there's a woman at the front office who says she's Hope's mom. A Mrs. Wilderstein, I believe?"

"Bring her back," I said. I looked at Hope, and she gave me a reassuring nod of approval.

"Do you want me to leave you two alone?" I asked.

"No, stay here with me. I may need you here so she knows I'm telling her the truth," Hope said.

Mrs. Wilderstein rounded the corner. She looked at Hope with a discouraged look on her face, almost as if Hope was in the principal's office instead of a safe house. She tried to hide her disappointment and embarrassment from me. After all, last week she was the wife to Luther and mom to Hope. And today, her husband is in jail, and her only daughter is in a safe house. Despite the tragedy of it all, Hope needed her sympathy. Mrs. Wilderstein grabbed Hope's hand and walked her over to the couch. Looking her in the eye, she calmly requested her to speak, saying, "Tell me everything."

Hope was not dumb. She saw through her mom's false sense of compassion. Her mom lacked sufficient evidence, and she was in need of answers. Her husband had betrayed her trust, which was a crisis all on its own. And on top of that, her daughter had been sexually misused by multiple abusers and needed her now more than ever.

I realized this was out of my realm of professionalism. I was uncomfortable, and I needed Grace.

"I'll be right back."

I walked down the hall to the staff lounge and opened the door quietly, just in case they were on the phone. Dezzie was talking to someone on her headset. So I motioned to Grace to come out.

"Grace, Hope's mom is here. I'll work the hotline. You go help Hope."

"Thank you, Faith. You're right, I should be there. Please pray for us," Grace pleaded.

It's not the first time Grace has had to meet with a parent. It is, however, the first time she has met with a parent whose husband is guilty of trafficking her own daughter. I prayed that Grace would have the right words that consoled both of them. They are both clients in need of guidance. I prayed for Grace to have good listening ears and for Hope's mom to have sympathy and compassion. I prayed for Hope. What she needed right now was unconditional love.

"Dear Lord, shower Hope with unconditional love that only You can give. Help her, Lord. This could be a pivotal moment in her decision to follow You. She needs reassurance that you are with her. She can't give up. We can't lose Hope."

When my shift was over, I walked to Grace's office to get a report on how the session with Hope's mom ended. The door was closed with her "Do not Disturb" sign hanging on the doorknob. As curious as I was, I just had to keep praying for them. As I walked into the foyer, I saw Dad, in uniform, talking to Oliver. "Hey Dad, what's going on?"

"Faith, is Mrs. Wilderstein here?" he asked in his investigator voice.

"Yes," I answered. "She's in Grace's office talking to Hope. She just got here about fifteen minutes ago."

"We need to take her into the station for questioning," he said. "I need to talk to both of them separately."

I walked Dad back to Grace's office and knocked, saying, "Grace, it's Faith and Officer Joule. Can we come in, please?"

Grace opened the door, and Dad introduced himself to Mrs. Wilderstein. Hope wasn't expecting the police to show up again, and I could see the concern in her face as she started to cry. Acknowledging Hope first, he said, "There's nothing to be afraid of, Hope. I'm just following protocol. I need to ask you and your mom some questions."

Cooperating with the police was Mrs. Wilderstein's best chance of getting her own questions answered. She surrendered, saying, "Yes, whatever we need to do to keep Hope safe."

After Dad confirmed Mrs. Wilderstein's identity, he ushered me to the door, saying, "Faith, go ask for Officer Diamond and bring him back here." He could see that I didn't want to leave. Looking me in the eyes with authority, he said, "Go on, we'll take good care of them."

Stepping out of the room, my heart raced. I did not want to leave Hope. Petitioning for wisdom for all of them and myself, a sense of the Holy Spirit overwhelmed my emotions. The Lord bestowed upon me a peace that I had not felt in ages. Standing outside of Grace's office, tears streamed down my face. They weren't tears of sorrow or anger. They were tears of awe at the evident work that the Lord was doing at that moment. Dezzie and I committed to this journey so many years ago, unaware of God's ultimate plan. Yet, God knew. All He required of us was surrender and obedience. All He asked was for us to sow seeds and nurture them. All He demanded was our purity of heart, mind, and body. He has orchestrated everything else. We are securely held in the palm of His hand. And then I heard His voice whisper, "It's going to be alright. Never lose Hope."

CHAPTER 20

CONFIDENT FAITH

The next day, my mind was consumed with thoughts of Hope. I wondered how her conversation with her mom unfolded. What did the investigation find that we didn't already know? I couldn't calm the whirlwind of thoughts swirling inside my head. After a full day of classes, I drove straight to the safe house.

On the drive over, I called to let Grace know I was on the way. As I entered, I saw Oliver sitting behind the plexiglass window waving me in. The door unlocked automatically. "Hey Faith, how's my favorite youngest sister doing today?" Oliver greeted me with a touch of Southern charm.

"I'm good, Oliver. Thank you for asking. How about you?"

Oliver, who had known me my whole life, picked up on my subtle clues-a slight swaying of my shoulders, a tapping foot. Like a caring brother, he understood I wasn't in the mood for a lengthy conversation. Aware that my thoughts were on our new resident, he offered, "If you're looking for Hope, she was in Grace's office."

I briskly walked down the hallway to the rear of the building. Approaching Grace's office door, I saw the elegant black and white sign hanging by a braided rope of twine on the doorknob: "In Session, Do Not Disturb." Despite the sign, I knocked gently on the half-opened door.

"Who is it?" Grace asked

"It's me, Faith," I answered, "Can I come in?"

Grace welcomed me in. She was sitting in the newly upholstered, yet recycled, robin's egg blue wingback Queen Anne chair beside the couch. Hope sat on the matching chenille sofa while I maneuvered the white leather rolling office chair to face them both.

Hope glanced up at me, her eyes wide as she took a deep breath. "We were discussing my mom," she began. "Faith, I don't know what to do." Pausing to collect her thoughts, Hope continued, her gaze shifting to the floor, "I should have told her sooner," she admitted, her voice heavy with regret. "It's just that I didn't know how to bring it up. I've rehearsed it thousands of times, but I've always been paralyzed by fear, especially of Luther's threats looming over me."

After a lengthy pause, she confessed, "I've often wondered how Mom would react if she knew the extent of Luther's double life. They were childhood friends, you know, living their best life as a married couple with big dreams of their future, growing old together. I feel like an intrusion to their marriage, an adopted kid who they've only known for a few years. If it weren't for me, none of this would have ever happened."

Grace and I sat in silence, giving Hope the space to process her thoughts. The weight of the quiet room became too heavy, and

Hope began to speak, unable to hold back her words any longer. "I'm still shocked by her reaction," she confessed. "I truly believed she would be devastated. I pictured her bursting in emotionally, running in to embrace me and never letting me go. I expected immediate hugs and tears, but it wasn't like that at all. I felt like she was crying more for her own sake than mine. I've never seen that expression on her face. It was like she couldn't bear to look at me. In fact, she confirmed my own worst thoughts about myself. I feel dirty. No matter how long I bathe or how many showers I take, I'll never be clean. I don't think she'll ever speak to me again. I mean, why would she?"

Then, without prompting, her voice trembling with self-condemnation, she answered her own question, "I'm repulsed at myself. I'm nothing but trash."

I moved to offer comfort, but Grace intervened, holding up her hand and shaking her head. "No," she murmured softly.

Hope needed to express herself without interruption. She talked as if she was just in the room by herself, just her and her thoughts.

"She's disappointed in me," Hope continued, her words heavy with anguish. "She's treating me more like a stranger than a daughter. Honestly, she showed me more kindness when she was my foster mom than she did yesterday."

Then, remembering that we were in the room, she looked at me and said, "Faith, you're not going to believe this. She actually asked me not to tell anyone."

Taking a deep inhale before she asked her next question.

"Can you believe that was the first thing on her mind?"

Shaking her head in disbelief, she reiterated, "I promised her that the safe house staff and the police were the only ones who know. I assured her that you wouldn't tell anyone."

Hope lowered her gaze, lost in contemplation. As she continued to replay the conversation with her mom in her mind, her agitation grew stronger. With tears streaming down her cheeks, she blurted out, "How can she be so selfish? I can't understand how she's worried about her own reputation at a time like this." Then, she loudly shouted, "Doesn't she realize that I need her now more than ever? This is not about her. This is about me."

We allowed her tears to flow freely, passing her the box of tissues. Then, we heard Gabby, the dog. She was whimpering and scratching outside Grace's door.

"Hope, do you like dogs?" I asked. "Gabby is worried about you. She hears you crying, and she wants to console you. Can we let her in?"

Hope nodded her head "yes" as she wept.

Gabby, our Bright Light Safe House pet, licked Hope's tears and hopped up on the couch, curled up beside her, and laid her head on Hope's knee.

I nodded in understanding, empathizing with her emotions. She composed herself and wiped away her tears. After blowing her nose, she looked at us with red eyes and posed a question, "Why are adults so secretive? She's a nurse, for goodness sake. She should know how to care for me. It's as if she doesn't even believe me. I tried to give her a hint when all of this was happening. I told her I didn't want her to work out of town anymore, but she insisted. I begged her not to leave this last time. She dismissed me, saying I was acting like a toddler, and told me to 'Grow up.'"

Then, Hope looked at me, her eyes filled with a mixture of longing and curiosity. "Faith, you're lucky your dad is a policeman. He was the first phone call you made when I ran here. You trust him, and he immediately believed you. What is it like to have parents to help you deal with this?"

I looked at Grace for permission to speak. She held out one hand facing me like a stop sign as if to say, "I know you want to help, but just wait."

Hope talked through her tears, expressing her deep despair, "If my mom sends me back to foster care, I'll just end it all. I have no family, no real home. There's nothing left for me to live for. I just want to disappear off the face of the earth."

She doubled over, burying her face in her hands as if to disappear into her tears. Grace tilted her head to one side, eyebrows raised, nodding her head, silently indicating that I could speak. I took a deep breath and exhaled slowly. I wanted to help Hope by sharing more of my story, but I didn't want to overshare. She had heard most of my life story yesterday. Another recollection of "The Life of Faith" might not be what she needed right now. After all, I wasn't a licensed professional counselor like Grace was. But I couldn't shake the feeling that I needed to say something. This was too important to ignore. So, despite my hesitations, I gathered my thoughts and looked up determined to offer what support I could.

Grace nodded again, encouraging me to share. "Go ahead, Faith. Tell Hope the rest of your story."

CHAPTER 21

FAITH SHARES FORGIVENESS

ope didn't even look up. Her head still resting in her hands, she was sobbing.

Despite her anguish, I spoke, hoping that, even in her pain, my words would provide some solace. "Hope, your hurt right now matters. It's real, and it stinks. And I'm so sorry for your pain. My story and yours hardly compare. You've been through so much worse. But our parents' reactions are very similar. It may surprise you, but my parents didn't want to talk about my hurt either. In fact, my mother never once mentioned it. Either my dad never said anything to her about it, or she chose to ignore it. But either way, I take full responsibility. After all, I lied to my dad and told him I was okay. I never told him the whole truth. My dad's initial angry outburst was so volatile that I didn't want to make him any more angry than he already was.

"In fact, over time, I became a good actress, skilled at pretending that nothing ever happened. I kept quiet for the sake of peace in my family.

"I had to put on a happy face, and pretending to be happy became better than dealing with reality. By suppressing my emotions for the sake of secrecy, I inadvertently buried them deeper in the recesses of my memory. They became so deep, I almost forgot about them.

"However, as I grew older, and the more I advocated for children, I realized it was imperative that I address the initial pain. My therapist and I had to go back to move ahead in the healing process. It became clear that discussing the past was necessary for forgiveness and freedom from the bondage that trauma held on me.

Hope, uninterested in delving into the psychological discussion, sat straight up, wiping her tears, and asked me, "Faith, did your parents EVER discuss it with you?"

"Yes, my dad did. He talked to me about it four years ago. I was staying home during spring break of my freshman year in college. I was overwhelmed with every part of my life, from school, relationships, lack of sleep, and grieving a bad breakup with a long time boyfriend. I was tired and struggled with thoughts of suicide. At that moment, I concluded that my dad and Jesus were the only men I could trust on this earth. What was the purpose of living if I had to live alone? I didn't want to grow up to be a bitter old maid, or at least that was my thinking.

"I chose to go see another counselor since Grace knew so much about my past already. I wanted an objective point of view. During the sessions, my counselor sensed that I might be holding back information from her. She suspected something deeper in my past. However, I denied it at the time. I wanted help, but I didn't want to do the work I truly needed to do. My emotions could no longer stay suppressed and started to boil over. One day, I exploded all over my dad.

"I was juggling so many new emotions as a college student with more responsibilities on my own. Not only was I unhappy with myself, but Dad seemed discontented with my progress at school. I was doing the best I could, but I lacked focus.

"I was in the middle of making a smoothie when he came back in the kitchen to get a mid-morning cup of coffee. He casually inquired about my plans for the rest of the day, and before I knew it, we were in an argument about whether I should work during my spring break. We rarely ever argued, so I was bewildered by the sudden surge of anger within me. I recognized the beginnings of an emotional eruption, and I was starting to quake. My heart felt unusually turbulent, like a dormant volcano awakening. My palms began to sweat. My pulse quickened. I could feel the heat rising within me. In my frustration, I couldn't help but snap back with a sassy remark, suggesting, 'Maybe I'll check with Dezzie about reviving the Daddy's Angels. I'm sure someone around here needs us. We could exchange babysitting or yard work for donations to our college fund. But first, I'm going for a run. Bye Dad, have a good day.'

"Out the door I bolted, feeling a rush of relief. 'Phew! I almost blew up back there!' I muttered to myself as I ran, picking up the pace to release some pent-up frustration. Speaking aloud to myself, I questioned, 'Why can't I just be confident and content instead of worrying about what he thinks? I'm not splurging on a beach trip; I'm just staying home, taking it easy. For goodness sake, I need to prioritize myself for once. Lord, what does he expect from me?'

"As I rounded the corner to the next block, that inner voice urged me, 'Faith, he's your dad. Go back and be honest. Tell him how you really feel.'

"With a bit of self-talk, I managed to calm my racing heart, and I retraced my steps back to the kitchen door. There stood my dad, gathering his sunglasses and keys. Before he could ask why I came back so soon, I mustered up the strength to speak the truth, saying, 'Dad, I'm going through a really tough time right now. I'm so angry that sometimes I feel like I just want to give up. I know it might be hard for you to understand, but I would really appreciate it if you could try.'

"In a defensive tone, he asked, 'What are you talking about?'

"I knew he wouldn't accept my sadness easily. He doesn't deal with emotions very well. Summoning my courage, I dared to ask the question that had weighed on my mind for so many years. 'Dad, why didn't you arrest him that night that he came into my room?'

I voiced the fear that had haunted me every day for the past six years. As soon as I said it, I wanted to stuff it back in. But it was out in the open, so I elaborated, 'I've spent every day since then terrified that he would come back. Don't you understand? That's why I used to lock my door. But it seems that you don't want to acknowledge that,' I added.

I looked down and spoke quietly but firmly, 'That's why I'm seeking help from someone who can understand and support me.'

'Faith, how long have you felt this way? You should have told me,' Dad's tone was laced with denial.

"'Dad, I have felt this way since that night when you found him in my room six years ago. You were so angry that I lied and told you that he didn't do anything. But you're a policeman. You had to have had a suspicion. You didn't even question me or him any further. I trusted that you knew best, so I retreated to my room, alone. I needed you. I wanted a hug, a shoulder to cry on. It was devastating. Don't you remember? Bianca went to the hospital that night and died two days later. I had to be strong for Dezzie and myself. It was so much for me to bear at that age. And now that I'm getting older, something is stirring inside of me, and I need to get help. In fact, you should know that I have been seeing a counselor.'

'Faith, your mom and I had a tough upbringing. We never went to counseling. We turned out fine. Professional help costs way too much. We just don't have that kind of extra income,' Dad responded.

'I expected you would say that,' I replied, feeling a mix of frustration and determination. 'I don't need money to see this counselor. I just want your permission to tell someone about that night so I can process it and figure out how to move forward.'

"Dad looked down at the floor, his expression reflecting the weight of the moment. He was grappling with how to navigate parenting me, his young adult daughter, who was on a journey to find her identity.

"'Dad this is not a reflection of you or your parenting. It's not about you. Please don't make this personal. I need to do this for me and my future. Please, Dad. Please release me from this locked room that I'm in. I can't explain it, but it's real, and it haunts me. Can I please have your permission to talk about that night privately with a professional therapist?' I pleaded desperately.

"'Please let me go,' I implored, waiting for his response.

"Dad, remained silent. His thoughts weighed heavily in the room.

"Feeling a nudge from the Holy Spirit, I sensed that this was my chance to convey what Jesus wanted him to hear. It was time to tell him that he was forgiven. I needed to relieve him of the weight of the guilt or shame that he might have been carrying.

"'I love you, and I want you to know that I have never blamed you for what happened that night. It's not your fault, and there's nothing you could have done to prevent it,' I explained gently, allowing my words to sink in.

"As he remained silent, the weight of the conversation hung heavily in the air and the absence of his response felt like a deafening silence to my heart. I hated seeing my dad upset.

"Pressing on, I reached out to him. "Dad, please look at me. I never wanted you to carry any guilt for what happened," I reassured him.

"Slowly, he raised his head and met my gaze with those big olive eyes of his.

"His admission caught me off guard. 'I didn't know that night still bothered you. Faith, you've never even mentioned it, so I didn't realize that we needed to discuss it,' he expressed earnestly.

"Through the tears streaming down my cheeks, I began to speak, my voice trembling with emotion. 'I didn't think about it for a long time. Somehow, I blocked it from my mind,' I confessed. "'But recently, during my Child Psychology class, the professor's lecture on dissociation from childhood trauma struck a chord with me. She talked about how we mentally dissociate from memories, feelings, or even a sense of identity.'

"'I've always felt like something changed in me at twelve years old, but I brushed it off as hormones and puberty,' I continued, my words pouring out as I recounted my realization. 'As I delved into our research paper on dissociation, it felt like I was on a wild search for more than words on a page. It was as if I was searching for a part of myself that I had long forgotten. The memories started to resurface slowly at first, but then they started to flow more clearly. I can't stop thinking about it. I need to confront it. I need to heal completely. And I need to be free from it.'

"Once more, he was left speechless, his silence speaking volumes. Desperately, I continued, my words pouring out in a rush of emotion. 'It's like God is pulling me closer to Himself, Dad, and He's asking me to take a leap of faith. He wants me to trust in Him to guide me through this journey. Dad, this is my next step to aligning with God's will for my life.'

"'You'll be relieved to know that the seminary in town has a school for family counselors,' I added, trying to offer reassurance. 'They only charge a donation from clients. I'll give them whatever cash I have in my wallet from babysitting jobs.'

"Yet again, he said nothing, leaving the weight of the moment hanging between us.

"'Jesus loves you, Dad. He forgave you a long time ago. He doesn't blame you for what happened. And neither do I,' I affirmed, my voice steady with conviction.

"Dad walked over to me and wrapped me in a long, comforting hug. Then, he stepped back, held my shoulders with his strong hands, and spoke softly, 'I'm sorry that I haven't always been the father you needed me to be. Will you please forgive me?'

"Tears of relief and gratitude streamed down my cheeks at his heartfelt words. 'I meant every word, Dad,' I affirmed. 'I do want to follow in your footsteps. Not only have you committed your whole life to enforcing the law, but now you're passing on your knowledge to others, teaching them how to protect and serve. You're a beacon of light, inspiring the young rookies to prevent crime and make a positive impact. You're the guiding light in our Bright Light Safe House.'

"His face beamed with a humble smile. He pulled me in for another hug, saying, 'Faith, it seems that you, my dear daughter, are teaching me. I have to get back to work, but I want to help you get through this. I trust that you are doing what's right for you, and I give you my blessing to go to counseling.'"

CHAPTER 22

A PRAYER FOR HOPE

Concluding my story with Hope, I said, "Talking to my dad in the kitchen that day marked a turning point in my healing journey. Being honest with him allowed me to move forward without the weight of fear. Respecting my father was very crucial, and I couldn't postpone that conversation any longer. Confronting truths and facing difficult conversations are essential steps towards healing. It's like dealing with a garbage can full of old food. We can try to mask the smells with air freshener or scented candles to try to cover the smell, but what we need to do is take out the garbage and wash out the bin. I had to remove the looming negativity in my life, and once I did, I started focusing on the positive in my life."

"So you think my mom will help me get through this?" Hope asked.

Grace consoled her, saying, "Hope, as difficult as it seems, I encourage you to have patience with your mom. Give her time to work through this grief that she's experiencing. I'm not giving her any excuses, but she's got her own concerns and questions. Not only is she losing a husband, but also a life that she once knew. We will work with you both to navigate all of the levels and layers of healing. Here at the Bright Light Safe House, we've seen the common patterns of parents' initial responses. No parent is completely prepared for abuse to happen to them or their family, therefore no one knows how to respond perfectly. Parents don't initially accept the abuse as real. It's easier to deny it than accept it. It's personal. We are a huge part of our parents' hearts, so they take on shame and regrets. And, yes, they are human, and their flesh is concerned about what others will think. Hope, let us help you and your mom. One thing we can promise you: we are here for you and your family."

Grace looked at the clock and said, "It's 4:20. Chapel starts in ten minutes."

I spotted Dezzie through the glass on the door, talking on the crisis hotline.

"I'm late for my shift," I mumbled, pointing to my watch.

I didn't realize how fast time had gone by. I gave her a non-verbal, "Are you okay?" with my thumbs up, and she gave me a reassuring thumbs up back, indicating that she was okay. I looked at my phone and pointed to it. I texted her, "I'm going to chapel with Hope. Please text me if you get busy, and I'll come back to help."

The Chapel is my favorite room in the Bright Light Safe House. Before our dads renovated the church, they researched "tranquil spaces." There were all kinds of websites that popped up with soothing colors, natural elements, soft lighting, textures, scents, and relaxing designs. Together, Grace, Dezzie, and I chose paint colors that reflected our favorite places and things. I appreciated our fathers involving us in the Bright Light Safe House plans. Their excitement in renovating the church sanctuary was reminiscent of the Bright Light treehouse construction just 10 years prior. We worked as a team to make this very special room a welcoming space for girls to worship and find healing.

We referred back to the Old Testament readings of God's plan for King Solomon's temple. We figured King Solomon had followed God's plan thoroughly when he built the temple, so maybe we could find some wisdom for our chapel, too. Since the Bright Light Treehouse was nestled in Old Solomon's branches, we wanted his Old Testament prayer of dedication somewhere in the chapel. When Solomon dedicated his temple, he prayed that God would change hearts.

"That's where your mom and I got the motto for our family, Faith. Remember the cross, the triangle and the heart? Jesus changes hearts. That's been our prayer for our family for over thirty years now," Dad had said.

So, King Solomon's prayer of dedication of the temple was painted on the wall in the rear of the chapel. It reads,

"Solomon's Prayer of Dedication
I Kings 8: 56 - 61

"Praise be to the Lord, who has given rest to his people Israel just as he promised. Not one word has failed of all the good promises he gave through his servant Moses. May the Lord our God be with us as he was with our ancestors; may he never leave us nor forsake us. May he turn our hearts to him, to walk in obedience to him and keep the commands, decrees and laws he gave our ancestors. And may these words of mine, which I have prayed before the Lord, be near to the Lord our God day and night, that he may uphold the cause of his servant and the cause of his people Israel according to each day's need, so that all the peoples of the earth may know that the Lord is God and that there is no other. And may your hearts be fully committed to the Lord our God, to live by his decrees and obey his commands, as at this time."

Before Hope and I took our seats, I toured her around the newly renovated room. I inhaled the new paint scent. The most beautiful parts of the room were salvaged from the original building. These bursts of colors from the original stained glass windows depicted the story of Jesus as you moved around the room. Starting with the back left of the room all the way around to the right rear of the room, each window seemed to radiate light that glowed to illuminate the sanctuary. From the birth of Jesus under the glorious stars, to the resurrection of Jesus and the open tomb with the morning sunrise, each window had an element of natural light that illuminated each picture.

The center window set at the peak of the gable in the front of the room reveals the character of Jesus and His light as a sun shines over Jesus with a child and a lamb. In Matthew 18:1, Jesus's disciples ask Him who will be greatest in the kingdom of Heaven. In verse two, He calls a child over to Him and tells them, "Truly I tell you, unless you change and become like the little children, you will never enter the kingdom of Heaven. And in verse four, He says, "Therefore, whoever takes the lowly position of this child is the greatest in the kingdom of Heaven. And whoever welcomes one such child in my name welcomes me."

"Jesus really loves children, doesn't he?" Hope whispered as if Jesus might hear her and answer her himself.

"Yes, He does. He loves you, too, Hope," I whispered back to her. She smiled.

The wisteria painted along the ceiling reminded us of the never-ending growth we have through Jesus, spreading the beauty of His love all around us. The chairs were comfortably spaced, with a small pull-out tray table attached to the back of each chair in front of us, much like an airplane. Our dads know how we girls like to jot down copious amounts of notes during a sermon, so the trays served as a small desk, complete with a notebook and a pen attached.

The residents started walking in just as Hope and I had walked all the way around the chapel. The girls are aware that chapel is an option before supper every Wednesday. It's only thirty minutes long, from 4:30-5:00. The girls can come with prayer requests and praises written on a small card to submit at the end of Grace's devotional. It's more like a small group and less like a church service. The girls are welcome to interact and answer questions aloud as Grace prompts them. Today, to our complete surprise, all of the residents attended. The chatter in the room was louder than usual, and we weren't quite prepared for what happened at the end.

Grace took her spot at the front of the room elevated on the platform. She welcomed everyone and prayed, "Dear Jesus, thank You for accepting us and loving us as our Heavenly Father, giving us a new family here at the Bright Light Safe House. Amen."

Grace looked out over the crowd and asked us, "Is everyone here today?"

Everyone looked around the room. Indeed, everyone was at Chapel.

"Well, I'm so glad you're all here. Today, I'm going to talk about rooms. You each have a room here that was carefully planned with you all in mind. Even though we didn't know you personally, we knew that you would appreciate a certain kind of room. We chose calm colors and modest decorations. We researched and toured other safe houses as we prepared these spaces for you. Unfortunately, many of you have sad memories of rooms that you have stayed in before. So, these rooms here are designed to help you rest and to make you feel safe. Today, I want to tell you about a room that you will live in forever in your Heavenly Father's house."

I saw a few heads shaking and a few girls whispering to their neighbor sitting beside them. Grace read from the Bible, and she had the scripture on the projector, "I'll read from John chapter fourteen, verse two. Jesus tells his disciples, 'In my Father's house are many rooms; if it were not so, I would have told you. I am going there to prepare a place for you.' (NIV)

"Did you know that the name of this church before we bought it was The Father's House? I'm sure when they built it over sixty years ago, they never imagined that it would be a real house for girls such as yourself, but God knew. Much like these rooms were prepared for you here in this house, Jesus is in Heaven preparing your eternal room."

Grace scanned the room, made eye contact with the girls, paused, and then repeated that last sentence for effect, "Jesus is in Heaven preparing your eternal room." Then she kept teaching, "We'll all be family in our Father's house one day. What do you think your room will look like there?"

One of the girls said, "It will be beautiful!"

Another girl responded, "I hope my room is pink."

"I hope I have my own bathroom," a voice came from the back.

Hope leaned over to me and said, "Do you really think I'll have a room in God's house?"

I looked at her and smiled.

Then, Grace continued, "The Father's House will be perfect. The Bible tells us that there will be no more sadness. There will be no more suffering. There will be no more sin."

Then, emphasizing the words by speaking up, she guaranteed us this, "There will be no more hurt, sorrow, crying, or pain."

She read Revelation 21:4, "'He will wipe every tear from their eyes. There will be no more death or mourning or crying or pain, for the old order of things has passed away.' It sounds too good to be true, doesn't it? However, Jesus keeps His promises. We can have full faith and hope in His Word. In fact, He promises us in the next verse that we can trust Him at his word, saying in verse five, 'He who was seated on the throne said, "I am making everything new!"' Then he said, 'Write this down, for these words are trustworthy and true.' So John wrote them down over 2,000 years ago for you and for me.

"What about the here and the now? What about today? We continue to pray for God's will to be done on earth as it is in Heaven. Do you believe that we can have glimpses of Heaven on earth? This place, for me, here with you all, is Heaven on earth. We are all here healing until the ultimate healing. Even though we are not sick with a fever or a disease, we are allowing our minds and hearts to heal from the hurt we have endured.

"Guess what else is not in Heaven? There is no hunger in Heaven. Until that day, we will take care of the body God has given us.

"At this time, if you haven't already, take a prayer card and fill it out. It's time to take prayer requests. If you have a card filled out, bring it up to the stage."

On any given Wednesday, there are only a few people who will submit a prayer request. One by one, each girl got up, walked to the front, and placed their card in Grace's hand. Thirty people came forward to hand Grace a card. Looking down at each card as they came to the front, Grace had a surprised look on her face. Something was different about these prayer requests.

Grace asked Hope to come to the platform, saying, "Hope, will you please join me up here?" Looking out at the girls, then at Hope, she declared, "It is obvious that Hope has become somewhat of a hero here at the Bright Light Safe House. This is the first time all the residents have attended chapel, and it's the first time they all had the same prayer request." Grace held up all the cards, announcing, "One name appeared on each girl's prayer request card. Her name is Hope."

Hope stood up and looked around at everyone. As she walked forward to the stage, Grace announced, "Hope, your courage has won the respect of your kingdom sisters in this room. Your journey so far has been one of fearlessness, armed with supernatural, heavenly strength. You are protected by a force much stronger than any coward or abuser out there. We stand here in unison, praying for you and your future."

A round of applause burst out among the girls, and they all stood up for Hope. After the applause faded, Grace turned to Hope and spoke, saying, "Hope, you're not alone. You have a sisterhood of girls who are cheering you on. Everyone, please bow your heads, and let's pray."

"Dear Lord, thank You for this place where we can come together to worship You. Please help Hope to heal and to know that she has a room in Your house in Heaven. May You bless her, keep her, and make Your face shine on her. Give her peace. Help her to remember that she doesn't have to worry about tomorrow because You are a good Father, and You will provide all her needs. You love her and will never leave her nor forsake her. Help her to know that she is in the palm of Your hand, and You will never lose Hope. Thank You, Jesus, Amen."

ACKNOWLEDGEMENTS

To Brian Dixon, who leads the hope*books authors with unwavering dedication. Your encouragement was pivotal in moving me beyond the initial stages of this process. The open communication, education, coaching, guidance, grace, and consistent pushes to meet deadlines have been given generously and without reservation. I'll always remember the Hope*Story conference where Brian looked me in the eyes and said, "Finish the book." Thank You, I needed that.

To my hope*books authors and cohorts, thank you to the ones who have finished your project and to the ones who are almost there. Although we write in different genres and address diverse ideal readers, we are united in our mission to serve others. Your support and camaraderie are a joy to me.

To the Sarasota Seven, you hold a special place in my heart. I cherish our friendship deeply, from the early morning coffees to the front-row pew and late-night conversations. Our time together is precious, and I look forward to more conferences with you in the future.

To my Pinelake Church Small Group, thank you for praying for me years before the book began. Your prayers for intentionality, clarity, and my goals were vital.

Finally, to Lisa Bright Wilburn, my neighbor and childhood friend whose home was a sanctuary during our youth. This book is a testament to our friendship. To all of my friends and family who encouraged and prayed for me throughout this writing journey, from the bottom of my heart, I thank you.

Connect with Carrie

Email me at carrieonstayhigh@gmail.com.

You can follow my author life on Instagram @carriewattswrites, YouTube @CarrieWatts-tn2em, or on FB @ Carrie ON

Visit my website: www.carriewatts.com.